A reckless thrill went through her as she felt his reaction to their closeness. Clearly, she wasn't the only one affected by their kiss

"I, uh, didn't mean to make you uncomfortable," Lydia said.

"You did nothing wrong."

"Well, you did want to stop." She hesitated, struck by a sudden thought. "I misread your signals, didn't I?" She pressed her palms to her cheeks as she backed away.

He closed the distance between them in two strides. "Lydia, you didn't misread anything." He angled his head to look into her eyes. "Listen, you've gone through a major upheaval in your life and I don't want to add to it. Believe it or not, I'm trying to protect you."

Derek struggled not to reach for her. He'd known how she lived, and he'd felt the innocence of her kisses but he hadn't wanted to carry the thought through to its logical conclusion.

Now he did.

Dear Reader,

October is a funny month in New York City. Sometimes it rains, sometimes it snows, sometimes it's sunny. And in the stores, there's the anticipation of Halloween with candy and costumes. Although children don't usually trick-or-treat in my building, I still buy candy and wear a witch's hat just in case. Maybe this year, a group of goblins and vampires will show up so that I won't have to eat a whole bag of chocolate myself. Speaking of vampires, October is a banner month for our readers. We've got enough paranormal and adventure so that you'll want to keep a light on at all times.

New York Times bestselling author Sharon Sala returns to the line with *Rider on Fire* (#1387), which features a biker chick heroine who is led on a mystical journey to her long-lost father. Of course, she finds true love on her quest…and danger. RITA® Award-winning author Catherine Mann continues her popular WINGMEN WARRIORS miniseries with *The Captive's Return* (#1388), where an airman finds his long-lost wife. As they race to escape a crime lord, will they reclaim their passion for each other?

You'll love Ingrid Weaver's *Romancing the Renegade* (#1389), the next book in her PAYBACK miniseries. Here, a sweet bookworm is swept off her feet by a dashing FBI agent, who enlists her aid in the recovery of lost treasure. Make sure to wear your garlic necklace with Caridad Piñeiro's *Temptation Calls* (#1390), in which a beautiful vampire falls for a mortal man. And while she's only known men as abusive, will this dashing detective tempt her out of the darkness? This story is part of Caridad's miniseries THE CALLING.

Have a joyous October and be sure to return next month to Silhouette Intimate Moments, where your thirst for suspense and romance is sure to be satisfied. Happy reading!

Sincerely,

Patience Smith
Associate Senior Editor

Please address questions and book requests to:
Silhouette Reader Service
U.S.: 3010 Walden Ave., P.O. Box 1325, Buffalo, NY 14269
Canadian: P.O. Box 609, Fort Erie, Ont. L2A 5X3

INGRID WEAVER

Romancing the Renegade

INTIMATE MOMENTS™

Published by Silhouette Books

America's Publisher of Contemporary Romance

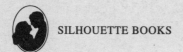 SILHOUETTE BOOKS

ISBN 0-373-27459-9

ROMANCING THE RENEGADE

Copyright © 2005 by Ingrid Caris

Books by Ingrid Weaver

Silhouette Intimate Moments

True Blue #570
True Lies #660
On the Way to a Wedding... #761
Engaging Sam #875
What the Baby Knew #939
Cinderella's Secret Agent #1076
Fugitive Hearts #1101
Under the King's Command #1184
Eye of the Beholder #1204
Seven Days to Forever #1216
Aim for the Heart #1258
In Destiny's Shadow #1329
†*The Angel and the Outlaw* #1352
†*Loving the Lone Wolf* #1369
†*Romancing the Renegade* #1389

Silhouette Special Edition

The Wolf and the Woman's Touch #1056

*Eagle Squadron
†Payback

Silhouette Books

Family Secrets
The Insider

INGRID WEAVER

admits to being a sucker for old movies and books that can make her cry. "I write because life is an adventure," Ingrid says. "And the greatest adventure of all is falling in love." Since the publication of her first book in 1994, she has won the Romance Writers of America RITA® Award for Romantic Suspense, as well as the *Romantic Times* Career Achievement Award for Series Romantic Suspense. Ingrid lives with her husband and son and an assortment of shamefully spoiled pets in a pocket of country paradise an afternoon's drive from Toronto. She invites you to visit her Web site at www.ingridweaver.com.

This book is dedicated to you, dear reader,
because you're the reason I write.
My heartfelt thanks.

Prologue

Arizona
Twenty-four years ago

The child took her hands from her ears. The only sounds left were the wind and the gritting hiss of sand against the boulders where Mommy had told her to hide. Was the bogeyman gone? She crawled through the shadow of the biggest rock and looked around the edge.

Sunshine glinted from the pieces of the truck that were scattered across the floor of the gully. The bushes wavered in the heat, but nothing moved except the flutter of black where her mother's skirt lifted in the breeze. The child stood. The pebbles hurt her feet—she'd lost her shoes—but she ran anyway. "Mommy!"

Her mother lay curled on her side, her back to the sun. Sand dulled her hair and stuck to her cheeks. She opened her eyes at the child's cry. "Hey, sweetie. There's my good girl."

The child dropped to the ground and threw her arms around her mother. "I want to go home now. Please, Mommy."

"Don't cry, sweetheart. Daddy's coming soon. He'll find us. You have to be brave a little longer."

She kissed her mother's cheek, but the sand stuck to her lips. She brushed it off the way Mommy did when she dried her tears. "I'm scared."

"Lie down with me, baby. We'll have a nap, okay?"

The child wasn't a baby, and she was too big for naps, but she snuggled closer anyway. Something was wrong with her mommy and she didn't know what to do.

"You'll be all right. Daddy will take you someplace safe and everything will be fine. I promise."

She pressed her face to her mother's shoulder and grasped one of her curls so she could rub it between her fingers. She did that when she was sleepy and Mommy read her a story. She wished this was a story in a book so it would end with everybody smiling and happy. She wanted to go home.

"I love you, baby. Remember that, okay? I don't want to leave you."

The words whispered across her face so softly, she had to hold her breath to hear them. She hiccupped, sending a tear into the corner of her mouth. "Mommy!"

"It's all right, sweet pea. You're a brave girl. A wonderful girl." She trembled. "Tell your daddy that I love him, too. I always will."

The kiss that touched her forehead was her mother's, but it was wrong. It wasn't like the good-night kisses that followed their bedtime stories. It was cold. So was the cheek that was pressed against her hair and the breath that puffed over her skin.

By the time the breath stopped, night had fallen and the child was too tired to cry. She was too young to grasp the scope of the tragedy that surrounded her.

Yet with an instinct as ancient as life, she understood that she didn't want to die.

Chapter 1

Colorado
Present day

Lydia Smith didn't want to die. That thought alone sure helped to put her other troubles into perspective.

"Please," she said. She heard the shaking in her voice and hated it, but what did pride matter when she was soaking wet and scared out of her wits? Rain battered the wall of pines to her right and nothing but darkness loomed beyond the guardrail to her left. No one except the three men who had forced her off this mountain road would hear her if she broke down and blubbered like a baby. "Please, let me go. I don't know where it is."

The man who stood behind her shook her by the arms hard enough to knock her glasses off her nose. "We'll let you go as soon as you tell us the truth."

"I'm telling you the truth. I don't know anything."

One of the other men rounded the front of the black van they'd been driving, his bulky form spotlit in the glare of its headlights. Like his companions, he was dressed in a green-and-brown camouflage jacket and wore his pant legs laced into his boots like a soldier.

"You want to reconsider that answer?" he asked.

"It's the only one I can give you." She squinted, trying to bring him into focus. Rain gleamed from his scalp through the short bristles of a buzz cut. He moved closer, and she saw the glint of metal in his hand.

Oh, God. He had a knife. Moisture sparkled from a long, curved blade. He pressed the knife flat against her throat. "Try again," he said.

Lydia fought the need to swallow. "You're making a mistake."

"Stop stalling." The man with the knife leaned closer, bringing with him the smell of sweat and motor oil. "Where did Zack hide the gold?"

"My father didn't tell me a thing. I swear. I don't know anything about the bullion robbery. I never learned who he really was until after he died."

The third man, the shortest one, smacked a baseball bat against his palm. It echoed wetly, the noise sounding more menacing than a clean hit. "You sure were in a hurry to get out of Denver. Looks to us like you were planning to go after it tonight."

"No. I couldn't. I—"

"Then where were you going?"

"I'm visiting friends," she lied. "They have a cabin near here. They expected me an hour ago and would be getting worried by now that I might have had an accident. They've probably already called the police."

The man who held her laughed. A wave of tobacco-scented breath wafted past her face. He gave her another shake. "If you wanted the cops, you should have thought of that before you ditched the tail they had on you."

Of course, she regretted her impulsive actions now, but at the time, she'd felt she had no choice. The desire to escape had been building for a month. With every visit from the police, each call from a reporter and flash of a camera, Lydia's urge to flee the fish bowl that was her life had strengthened.

But it was her father's headstone that had been the final straw. It had been erected yesterday. By this morning, someone had chiseled off a corner of the granite.

The chunk of stone was already being offered for sale on eBay. A genuine souvenir of the notorious Zachary Dorland Smith.

Cold metal pricked the skin beneath her jaw. Lydia clenched her teeth together to keep them from chattering.

"She's as sneaky as her old man, isn't she, Earl?" The man with the knife grabbed a handful of her hair and wound it into his fist to hold her head in place. Pain shot through her scalp as some of the roots pulled out. "She knows where it is, all right. She was waiting until the heat died down before she made her move. She thought she could use the cover of this storm to get past us."

"Yeah. Hey, Pete. I think we should give her some incentive to talk to us."

The short man grasped the bat with both hands and swung it toward her car. The back windshield smashed into a spiderweb of cracks. He swung it again and the glass shattered into a spray of tiny, glittering chunks. Some bounced across the trunk and clattered against the guardrail, but most of it poured into the back seat.

Lydia's eyes filled with tears. According to the police, her father's assailants had likely used a bat when they had broken his leg. They probably hadn't meant to kill him—he'd been ill for years, and it was his heart that had given out in the end. The horror of what he had endured before he'd died had been unimaginable to Lydia.

Until now.

These had to be the same men. They hadn't left Denver after all. They must have been biding their time, watching her house and waiting, just like the police and the media and the legions of treasure seekers.

And like everyone else, they wanted the secret that Zachary had taken to his grave.

Why, Dad? Why didn't you tell me? Didn't you realize what would happen?

She bit her lip, torn by the anger that tangled with her grief.

Yet how could she mourn her father when she had never really known who he was?

The short man, the one they had called Pete, turned away from her car and walked toward her. Her glasses snapped under his foot as he smacked the bat against his palm again. At the contact, water splattered outward from his hand, making her think of blood.

A soul-deep wave of terror swept through her. She strained against the hold on her arms. "No," she cried. "Please, don't hurt me."

"Tell us what we want to know."

"If I could, I would. You have to believe me. I don't want anything to do with my father's gold. I wish I'd never heard of it. You're welcome to take it all."

"Where is it?"

"I have no idea."

"You're lying."

"I'm not. I would tell you if I could, but *I...just... don't...know!*"

Her shout echoed through the darkness, as violent in its way as the sounds of the bat and the breaking glass. For a moment, no one moved. Then the man with the knife twisted the blade away from her throat. Wet metal slid along her cheek and touched the top of her ear. She heard a swift, ripping sound and the pressure on her scalp abruptly disappeared.

"Ever see a deer skinned, honey?" The knife flashed in front of her. Something long and dark swung across her vision. It took her a moment to realize that she was looking at a thick hank of her own hair. "I like to start at the head and work down."

A distant roaring filled her ears. Dear God, she didn't want to die. Not now. Not like this. If only she had stayed where it was safe. That's how she'd always lived. Safety above all else.

But regrets were as useless as pride. She'd known when she'd made the decision to flee her home that there would be no going back. The life she had known had ended a month ago, anyway. It was her chance at a new life that she didn't want to lose.

The man dropped her hair on the ground and took a step away. "Hell, Pete. We're going to have company. I thought you said no one came down here."

Lydia's pulse tripped as she finally focused on what she'd been hearing. The roaring in her ears had congealed into the sound of an engine.

Could someone be coming? Please, let them stop. Let them help. What she wouldn't give for just one of the cops or reporters or even a souvenir hound.

The grip on her arms tightened. She was dragged

backward, away from her car and closer to the van. She tried to dig in her heels but her sneakers skidded ineffectually over the gravel at the side of the road. "No!" she cried, jerking at her arms. "Let me go!"

"Keep her quiet, Earl," Pete ordered.

The man who held her—Earl?—shifted his grip, locking his arm around her neck and clamping his other hand over her mouth. She clawed at his sleeve, fighting to get air.

"Lose the knife, Ralph," Pete instructed, dropping his bat to the ground behind her car. "I'll do the talking."

The stocky man, Ralph, quickly sheathed his knife and slipped it into a pocket on the side of his pants. As he and Pete turned to face the road, Earl continued to drag her backward until they were beside the van.

Lydia strained to listen as the sound of an approaching vehicle gradually rose above the noise of the rain. Headlights flashed along the guardrail and reflected from her car. An engine rumbled closer. A few seconds later, the pitch of the motor changed to an idle and the twang of country music floated through the air.

"Hey there." It was a man's voice, deep and whiskey-smooth. The volume of the music dropped. "You boys need some help?"

"No. Everything's fine."

Lydia realized whoever had stopped wouldn't be able to see her any more than she could see him. She screamed against the palm that covered her mouth, but her cry was too muffled to carry over the sound of the music and the rain.

"Looks like you had an accident." The stranger's tone was easygoing, with the trace of a drawl. He could have been commenting on the weather instead of an obviously wrecked car.

"It's nothing," Pete said. "My friend here skidded and missed the turn. I'll drive him home."

Lydia twisted her head, trying to bite Earl's hand. He hooked his fingers under her chin to keep her jaw shut.

"That Volvo's a mess. You need a tow truck?"

"We'll handle it."

He paused. "Bad luck, blowing out the back windshield like that, seeing as how it was the front of the car that hit the guardrail."

"Yeah. Bad luck."

Lydia kicked backward and twisted against Earl's grip. He flexed his elbow around her throat, cutting off her air. Her vision blurred. She pounded his arm.

"I've got a friend who runs a body shop," the stranger said. "He could fix that windshield for you boys, no questions asked."

"We've got it covered."

"He'd give you a good deal. Hang on, I've got his card in here somewhere."

"Don't bother."

"You sure?"

"We like to mind our own business. If you're smart, you'll do the same."

"Whoa, no need to get testy." The music swelled, along with the sound of the engine. "Hope you boys enjoy standing around in the rain."

In desperation, Lydia swung her foot at the van. It hit the side with a loud clunk. She was able to get in three more solid kicks before Earl dragged her out of range. Surely, whoever was stopped on the road had heard that, she thought.

But evidently, he hadn't heard it. Or more likely he had, and had decided to ignore it.

The irony of the situation wasn't lost on her. After

four weeks of having her privacy invaded by everyone and their dog, she had to run into the one person in the country who didn't want to get involved in her affairs.

The vehicle moved off. Sooner than she would have believed possible, the noise of the engine was swallowed by the rattle of the rain.

No! Lydia thought. *Please, come back!*

"Grab the stuff from her car, Ralph," Pete said. "She might have a map or something."

"Sure thing, Pete," he replied. "I'll take a look."

"Any money you find goes to the Colonel."

"Aw, come on. We got a right to—"

"You know the rules."

Lydia glimpsed a ragged glow through her car's broken rear windshield as the dome light came on. She thought of the purse she'd left on the front seat, and the gym bag she'd tossed in the back. Not much to show for a lifetime, but it was all she'd been able to take out of her house without raising the suspicions of the people who watched.

While Ralph leaned through the door of her car, Pete retrieved his bat from the ground, propped it on his shoulder and turned to regard Lydia. "Better put her in the van before we get interrupted again, Earl."

"The bitch tried to bite me," he said, loosening his choke hold. "Where'd you put that duct tape?"

"It's in the back beside the toolbox."

Afterward, Lydia couldn't recall how it started. Everything happened so fast, she barely had the chance to register the sound of footsteps before Earl jerked backward with a grunt and the grip on her throat was torn away.

She staggered sideways, filling her lungs with air as she tried to regain her balance. She turned just in time to see Earl go headfirst into the guardrail beside her. His skull hit the steel with a resounding crunch and he crumpled to the ground.

Someone seized her by the shoulders and gave her a firm push toward the road. "Run! My Jeep's parked around the bend."

Lydia recognized the deep voice. It belonged to the stranger who had stopped earlier. He *had* come back. She scrambled as far as the blacktop before she realized she couldn't see where she was going.

She stopped and glanced over her shoulder.

The scene that was unfolding in the glow of the van's headlights was a blur of motion. Although most of the details were lost to her, she didn't need her glasses to be able to grasp what was happening. A tall, blond man spun toward Pete, pivoting on one foot and whipping his trailing leg forward just as Pete swung the bat.

The stranger's boot connected with Pete's jaw. The bat went flying end over end into the darkness beyond the guardrail. A split second later, Pete was propelled into the front of the van. His cry of surprise ended with a thump as his forehead hit the bumper.

"What the—" Ralph tossed aside her belongings that he'd brought out of her car and reached for the pocket on the leg of his pants.

"Look out!" Lydia called, running forward. "He's got a knife."

The warning had scarcely left her lips when the blond stranger dove to one side, rolled across the ground and sprang back to his feet with another graceful, spinning kick.

Metal clattered against her car. There was the smack of a fist against flesh, and the third man lay motionless beside her gym bag.

Lydia shivered, stunned by the speed of what she'd just witnessed. The relief that swept over her left her weak. She moved to the edge of the pool of light, hugging her chest, her entire body shaking. "Thank you," she said. "For coming back. I thought you hadn't realized what was going on."

At her words, the stranger turned to face her. He strode forward and caught her gently by the elbow. "Are you okay, ma'am?"

She nodded. "You got here before they could hurt me. Saying thank you hardly seems adequate, does it? But I don't have any experience with situations like this, so I wouldn't know the right thing to say." She tried to smile but her lips were trembling too badly and it turned into a grimace. "I'm sorry. I'm babbling. It must be the stress. Are you all right? Did they hurt you? I can't believe the way you were able to overpower all three of them like that. It was—" Her voice broke as she glanced at the crumpled bodies on the ground.

An image of horror, like the vague memory of a nightmare, stirred in the buried layers of her mind.

"Hey, you're not going to faint on me, are you?"

She took a deep breath and focused on her rescuer.

At first glance, his appearance matched the easygoing drawl she'd heard in his voice. He wore the scuffed boots, broken-in jeans and denim jacket of a cowboy. His frame was broad-shouldered and lanky. In spite of the impressive fighting skills he'd displayed seconds ago, and in spite of the rain that was pelting them both, his stance was relaxed. Everything about him was don't-give-a-damn casual.

Except for his smile. She was close enough to see that clearly, and there was nothing casual about the tight curl of his lips. It was primitive and dangerous, a feral grin of satisfaction, as if he'd *enjoyed* what he'd just done.

This man had just saved her life. She had no reason to fear him.

Yet it wasn't fear that was pounding through her blood now, was it? It was excitement. Adrenaline. A reaction to her escape from death.

And a reaction to this man.

Good God, was this excitement sexual? She must be falling apart.

"I hate to rush you, ma'am, but we need to get moving." He ducked his head to look into her eyes. "These boys are going to be pissed when they wake up and I don't much feel like being around when they do."

She nodded. "Yes, of course."

He glanced behind him, then stepped over Ralph's motionless form and scooped up the remains of Lydia's glasses along with her purse and her gym bag. "Are these things yours?"

"Yes. Thank you."

Holding her belongings under one arm, he loped toward the road, snagging her hand with his as he went by.

Lydia didn't normally trust strangers. Yet right now, if she wanted to survive her only option was to go with this man. She hesitated for no more than a heartbeat before she turned and ran with him down the road.

All things considered, she was taking it well, Derek Stone decided. For someone who had lived as sheltered a life as Lydia Smith, what she'd gone through tonight could have sent another woman into hysterics. But apart from the way her teeth were chattering, she was doing her best to hold herself together.

Then again, she hadn't yet seen what they'd done to her hair.

Damn, he'd never expected the Canyon Brotherhood to make a move on Zack's daughter so soon. He'd assumed they would hold off the same way he'd been doing, at least until she led them closer to the bullion. That attack was too sloppy to have been sanctioned by the Colonel—the team must have taken the initiative on their own.

Still, Derek had planned to make contact with her at some point, and he'd managed to do just that, so he might as well play the hand he'd been dealt. He put the Jeep into gear, spraying gravel from the wheels as he steered back onto the road.

"My cell's in the glove compartment," he said. "You can use it to call the cops."

She rubbed her palms briskly over the legs of her jeans. "If you don't mind," she said, "I'd rather not involve the police."

Of course, he'd known she would say that, but he didn't want to let on that he did. "Why not?"

"They won't do any good."

"I know it's none of my business, ma'am, but from where I stood, it didn't look as if you were handling things on your own all that well."

"I wasn't. I realize that. Those men might have killed me if you hadn't come along." She twisted her neck to peer out the back window, then looked at him. "You saved my life. Thank you. Really, it does sound inadequate, but I can think of no other way to express my gratitude. It must have taken tremendous courage to step in the way you did to rescue a complete stranger."

Derek concentrated on keeping the Jeep on the slick pavement as it fishtailed around the next bend.

Lydia was wired from adrenaline, her speech coming out too fast, but she had good reasons for her anxiety: the Brotherhood's usual policy was to leave no witnesses.

"Thank you so much," she said. "What you did was truly heroic."

Hardly, but it suited his purpose to let her believe that. Honesty wouldn't be the best approach right now. She had resisted a month's worth of direct questioning from the authorities and had narrowly escaped a brutal interrogation, so odds were she wouldn't be in the mood to cooperate when it came to the gold.

Worse, if she ran from him, she would be a sitting duck for another attack from the Brotherhood.

Derek didn't know her well enough to predict how she would react to the truth, so he wasn't going to risk it at this stage. She didn't need another interrogator; she needed a friend.

He lifted his thumb to his forehead as if tipping an imaginary hat and stole a glance at his passenger. "My pleasure, ma'am."

She tried to give him a smile.

Derek found himself staring. Lydia's photographs didn't do her justice. This wasn't the plain, bespectacled bookworm of a woman the media had dubbed the Million Dollar Mouse.

Etched in the glow of the dashboard lights, her features looked delicate, almost elfin, with a hint of pixie wildness lurking beneath the surface. Together with those doe-in-the-headlights eyes and all that luxurious dark hair—well, half her hair—in wet disarray around her shoulders, she was far more appealing than he could have anticipated. He couldn't see what kind of figure she had beneath her baggy jacket, but he suspected that even soaking wet, she couldn't weigh much over a hundred pounds.

Still, there was a surprising amount of spirit in her small frame. The fact that she'd bolted from Denver in the first place had taken everyone off guard. Then instead of running off the instant he'd freed her from those Brotherhood thugs, she'd stayed to shout a warning.

"And thank you for giving me a ride. My car..." Her voice wavered. "I know that Volvo was getting old, but it was a good, reliable car. I hope it can be fixed."

He returned his attention to his driving. "From the looks of it, those guys ran you off the road."

"Yes, they did. The first time they hit me, I thought it was accidental, because it was dark and the road was wet, but then they came up beside me and intentionally knocked me into that guardrail. The air bag hurt when it went off."

"Maybe you should see a doctor."

"No! I'm fine."

"Hey, take it easy. I'm concerned about you, that's all."

"I'm sorry I raised my voice. I do appreciate your help, but just because you rescued me, you're certainly not obligated to take care of me. I've never believed that proverb that says if you save a life you're responsible for it. Actually, I'm not a big believer in proverbs at all."

"Okay. No police and no doctor. What do you want me to do?"

She reached for the purse he had picked up and dug around inside it for a while. "If it's not too much out of your way, could you drop me off at the next town? I believe it's Leadville. I'll find someone to repair my car there. Perhaps you could give me the card of your friend who runs the body shop…oh, no!"

"What's wrong?"

"My cash. I had it in an envelope in this zippered compartment." She curled over her purse and rifled through it again. "It's gone. The man who took my things from the car must have stolen it."

"What about your credit cards?"

"I didn't bring any."

That was smart, he thought. The cops would have been able to trace her cards if she used them. "Did they get your ID?"

"No, it looks as if all they took was the money. Oh, God. I was so worried about those men hurting me that I hadn't given a thought to the possibility that they would steal anything." Coins jingled. She pulled out a handful of change, spread it out on her palm and tilted her hand toward the dashboard lights. "Ninety-five cents. That's all I have left."

"Sorry. I should have checked that guy's pockets before we took off."

"No, you couldn't have. We had to get out of there."

"I've got about sixty bucks on me." Derek took one hand from the wheel and leaned to the side so he could slip his wallet from his pocket. He offered it to her. "You can have it if that'll help."

"That's too generous. After everything you've already done, I couldn't possibly—"

"It'll be a loan, okay? Take it."

"Thank you," she said, her voice breaking. She opened his wallet, withdrew three tens and passed the wallet back to him. "I've taken thirty. I promise I'll pay you back as soon as I can."

"No problem. Where were you heading?"

She cleared her throat, reached into her purse again and drew out a pair of round, wire-frame glasses similar to the broken set he'd retrieved from the ground. Squaring her shoulders, she fitted the glasses on her nose as if she were donning armor. "Um, west."

Well, did he expect her to give him a straight answer? That would have been too easy.

She pressed closer to the door to look out the side mirror. Wet stubs from her butchered hair stuck out above her ear, yet she kept her chin angled stubbornly upward, as if preparing herself for the next blow fate might choose to deal her.

Derek had a sudden urge to pull her toward him and tuck her protectively under his arm. In spite of the brave front she was trying to project, he could see she was hanging on to her control by a thread.

He tightened his grip on the wheel until the urge passed. He was surprised he'd felt it at all—normally, it took more than this to stir up his emotions. But he couldn't afford to lose sight of his objective. Too much was riding on being the first to that gold.

"I know you said you wanted me to drop you off," he said, "but it doesn't seem right for me to just leave you on your own with only thirty dollars and ninety-five cents. Especially with a bunch of guys cruising around who like to mug lone women. Sure you don't want to call the cops?"

"I can't."

"Why not?"

She hesitated, fiddling with the arm of her glasses. "I don't want the police to know where I am."

He pretended to digest that for a while. And in fact, it did take him off guard. This was the kind of confidence he'd been hoping for, but he hadn't expected her to open up so soon. "Are you on the run?"

Her hesitation was longer this time. "Yes."

"From the cops or from those guys with the camo jackets?"

"I suppose I could say both."

He adjusted the wiper speed, keeping his movements casual while he gave a low whistle. "So that wasn't a random mugging?"

"No."

"Why are they after you? What did you do?"

"Me? I did nothing. Absolutely nothing."

"Okay."

"It's true."

"Sure."

She shook her head. "It's complicated."

"Try me."

She remained silent.

"By the way, my name's Derek Stone." He held out his right hand. "And if you don't want to see a cop, that's fine by me."

Still no response.

"Okeydokey." He moved his hand to the heater and switched the blower on high, then turned on the CD player and pressed Play. Merle Haggard came on, singing about beer. Derek lowered the volume, just in case Lydia decided to divulge anything else, although at this stage, he was more concerned with winning her trust than with getting information.

It was a strategy that had always worked for him back in his FBI days. Once he gained a subject's trust, the rest would inevitably follow on its own. Judging by her speech and body language, Lydia was still high on adrenaline and not thinking straight, but she was bound to crash soon. His best bet was to make sure he was there when that happened.

Lydia gasped and twisted to look behind them again. "Oh, my God. I see lights."

He glanced in the rearview mirror. A halo of light swung through the rain, illuminating the brush at the edge of the trees and the gravel at the shoulder. Seconds later, a set of headlights streamed around the bend.

Derek swore under his breath and stepped on the gas. Those guys must have been tougher than he'd thought—he'd counted on them being out for longer than this. He'd deliberately stopped short of killing them, since that would have caused too many complications, both with the Brotherhood and the cops. They were merely foot soldiers; he was after the man at the top.

"It's the same van!" she cried. "I can tell by the lights. They cracked that orange light on the passenger side when they slammed into my car the second time. Oh, no! They're gaining on us!"

"Not if I can help it. Hang on!" He wrenched the wheel to the right. The Jeep tilted alarmingly as it bounced across the loose rocks at the foot of the slope. Spruce boughs scraped the roof and the window beside Lydia, making her jerk backward.

Derek maintained a death grip on the wheel to keep the Jeep from rolling. It had been years since he'd taken a group backpacking through this area. If he'd miscalculated his position...

Ah, there was the track, right where it should be. His headlights picked out a dark gap in the trees. He steered directly for it, switched into four-wheel drive and gunned the engine.

"What are you doing?" Lydia shrieked.

"We're taking a shortcut."

She braced her feet against the floor and clutched the

dashboard. "I'm sorry for yelling again. This isn't fair to you. I never meant to get you involved in my problems. No, that's not right, I hoped you would get involved, but—"

"Too late, ma'am. Whatever you're into, we're in it together now."

Chapter 2

Lydia awoke to the sound of clunking and a tuneless whistling. For a groggy instant she thought she was still in Denver, snug beneath her duvet with the embroidered border of marching geese while her father puttered around the kitchen downstairs.

No matter how early she set her alarm, he'd always seemed to be up before her. She pictured him at the table, his favorite delft-blue cardigan buttoned over his paunch, his gray hair poking straight up at the crown of his head and in need of a trim. With his mug of coffee steaming at his elbow and his glasses balanced on the tip of his nose, he would be deep in his morning newspaper ritual.

It had never struck her as odd that Zachary had four newspapers delivered to the house every day. He was a great follower of current events. Nor did she wonder why he refused to set foot outside the door until he'd gone through every page.

She'd never found his aversion to being photographed as anything suspicious, either. He was her dad, so she had accepted his quirks without question.

The grief started to gather even before she opened her eyes. So many years, so many lies.

She rubbed her nose against the duvet, but instead of polished cotton, she felt coarse denim. And rather than the floral aroma of her fabric softener, she inhaled the scent of sandalwood and man.

She opened her eyes with a start. She wasn't in her bed or her house, she was in the front seat of Derek Stone's Jeep. He wasn't here, but her coat was spread across the steering wheel and his jacket was draped over her chest.

Memories of the night before flooded over her, bringing her fully awake. Where were they? They had bounced along Derek's so-called shortcut for miles after the headlights behind them had disappeared. The last thing she remembered, they had stopped in the middle of a stream and he had leaned over her to get a flashlight from the glove compartment, muttering something about the engine stalling.

It astounded her that she'd been able to fall asleep at all, but she must have been out for hours since it was already dawn, and her coat looked almost dry. She slid one hand over her slacks and her sweatshirt, and discovered only a trace of dampness along the seams.

She touched her nose to Derek's jacket again, taking a furtive whiff of his scent. It helped to steady her, pushing back the budding panic. He had rescued her, he'd offered to lend her money and now had covered her with his jacket. Could he really be as kind as he seemed?

She straightened her glasses and looked around. The windows were too fogged up to see through, so she cleaned off a circle from the side window with her palm and brought her face close to the glass.

They were in a small clearing—apparently, Derek had managed to get them out of the stream. An early morning tapestry of color expanded before her, as vivid as a postcard, from the yellow-green of a sloping meadow to the rich shade of towering evergreens that bordered it. The sunshine bore the crisp angle of September, slanting through the scattered fragments of yesterday's storm clouds and glittering from the wet treetops like gold.

Gold. If only it could be that easy to find.

The whistling came again, this time forming into a melody that sounded vaguely familiar. It was an Elvis song, "Good Luck Charm." Lydia wiped a swath of condensation from the front windshield and saw that the hood of the Jeep was raised. Derek must be working on the engine. Grabbing his jacket, she opened the door and climbed out.

He was leaning under the hood, his arms extended in front of him as he fiddled with some pie-plate-shaped cover in the center of the engine block. "'Morning, ma'am," he said without looking up. "How are you feeling?"

Stiff, damp and completely disoriented, she thought. "Fine, thank you. I can't believe I fell asleep."

"I can. It usually happens after adrenaline highs."

"Does it? I wouldn't know."

"Yeah. It's a natural rebound while your body recovers. I see it all the time in my line of work."

She pictured him on horseback, a Stetson tilted over his face as he reined in an unruly stallion or cantered after a stray cow. Or whatever cowboys did these days.

He fastened the top on the cover and glanced at her. "You handled yourself well, you know."

He was being too kind. She remembered shaking and babbling like an idiot. She held out his jacket. "Thank you for loaning me your jacket."

"It wasn't as wet as yours." He straightened from beneath the hood and turned to face her. "Better hang on to it until I get a chance to clean up."

Lydia hugged the jacket to her chest. She'd seen Derek Stone in the headlights of the van and in the glow of the dashboard lights, but seeing him in daylight was something else altogether.

She hadn't realized what a handsome man he was. The night's growth of dark blond beard stubble that shadowed his cheeks and jaw suited him, giving his face a rough-hewn, rugged air. His hair was thick and shot through with sun-streaked highlights. He must have combed it with his fingers—a lock fell over his forehead, making her itch to stroke it back and test its texture....

She cleared her throat. Noticing his looks was as silly as being affected by the scent of his jacket. "Did you fix the engine?"

"Probably." He took a rag that was spread over the fender and wiped his fingers. "I'll know for sure as soon as I try to start it."

"Do you think we lost them?"

"Those boys from the van? Yeah. They wouldn't have been able to follow us up here without a four-wheel drive."

She looked around, but she could see no trace of a road, only the muddy tracks the Jeep's tires had left on the meadow. They hadn't come far from the stream after all. It gurgled past a bed of boulders only a few yards behind them, providing a musical background to the chorus of awakening birds. "Not that I don't appreciate everything you've done, and no offense to your driving abilities, because they're quite formidable, but do you have any idea where we are?"

"Sure." He gestured to the mountain slope that rose beyond the treetops. "There's a road just on the other side of that ridge. The track we've been following joins up with it about six miles from here."

"Oh."

"Where do you want me to take you once we reach it?"

She hesitated. After everything he'd done for her, she didn't feel right about lying to him again. "Actually, that could be a problem. Those men are probably going to be looking for me."

"Yeah, I was thinking about that." He rubbed at some grease on his palm. "They did seem determined."

"I've put you in jeopardy as well. It's not fair that you're involved in my troubles just because you decided to be a Good Samaritan."

"I've handled worse characters than that."

She didn't doubt he could, she thought as she remembered the deadly skill he'd shown with his spinning kicks. Had he learned to fight like that in cowboy brawls?

It wasn't only his face that the daylight revealed more clearly. His body was equally impressive. Beneath the rolled-up sleeves of his chambray shirt, his forearms rippled with taut muscles. The way he stood, with one ankle crossed over the other and his weight shifted to one leg, he projected confidence and an easy animal grace.

A bird trilled from the trees. It was answered by another trill in the distance. Lydia glanced behind her. She could see no movement, other than the swaying of spruce boughs in the breeze. Whether there was a road on the other side of the ridge or not, they still appeared to be in the middle of nowhere.

And she was alone with a complete stranger, a man who'd demonstrated the physical prowess to overcome three men within seconds.

Shouldn't she be nervous? That would be the sensible reaction in these circumstances, yet Lydia knew the little bump in her pulse when she returned her gaze to Derek wasn't from fear.

He was a strikingly masculine man. Not the kind of person she would have had the occasion to encounter in her old life—rugged, cowboy, martial-arts experts didn't tend to frequent vintage bookstores—but as she'd already realized, that old life was over. She was starting a new one.

"Considering what you've been through, ma'am," Derek said, moving toward her, "I can understand that you didn't feel like talking last night. But if you don't mind, I'd like to know exactly what it is that I got into here. Why are those guys after you?"

Whatever you're into, we're in it together now.

She felt a twinge of guilt as she remembered what Derek had told her before they'd left the road. So far, he'd shown through his actions that he meant her no harm. It was the opposite. He'd put himself in danger in order to help her. She lifted her gaze to his.

His eyes were the deep blue of a mountain lake. His lashes were dark brown and sinfully thick, evoking a lazy sensuality that was echoed in the laugh lines that feathered across his tanned skin. The whole effect was so beautiful, it took her breath away.

"What's wrong?" he asked.

Aside from the fact that she was on the run for her

life, was in the middle of nowhere and was experiencing another jolt of sexual excitement? She didn't
think she could blame this one on adrenaline. "You're
really being very decent about all of this," she said.
"And you're right. The least I could do is tell you the
truth."

"The truth, ma'am?"

She pushed her glasses more firmly onto the bridge
of her nose, trying to gather her thoughts. If she could
see him this clearly, he'd be able to see her, too, so it
was only a matter of time before he recognized her,
anyway. Lord knew, her face had been in the papers
often enough. "I'm Lydia Smith."

"Pleased to meet you, Lydia."

She waited for the name to sink in. Over the past
month, she'd seen a wide variety of reactions, from
scandalized shock to prurient interest. Most of the time,
though, it was simply greed. Any second now he would
realize who she was.

One corner of his mouth lifted in a half smile that
brought out a dimple in his cheek. "I don't think I've
met a Lydia before. It's a pretty name."

Pretty? That threw her for an instant. Pretty wasn't
a word that she normally heard applied to her. Compe-
tent, yes. Efficient and dutiful, sometimes even pleasant on the rare occasions when she dressed up or went
to the trouble of putting on makeup, but never pretty.
She had no illusions about her looks.

Of course, he was only talking about her name. "My
father was Zachary Dorland Smith," she said.

"Okay."

"From Denver."

"Yeah? Is that where you were traveling from?
You're a long way from home."

She nodded, puzzled by his lack of comprehension. "That's why those men in the van were after me," she said. "They think I know where my father hid the gold."

His smile faded. "Whoa. I'm missing something here. What gold?"

"The gold bullion from that Federal Reserve robbery. You must have heard about it."

He shook his head. "I just got into Denver yesterday and was on my way home when I ran into you. I haven't had a chance to catch up on the news."

"It's been all over TV and the papers for the past month. Where on earth have you been?"

"Peru."

"What?"

"I took a group kayaking down the Colca. What's this about gold?"

She studied his reaction, but he still wasn't showing any signs of recognition. Either he was the world's best poker player, or he really hadn't heard what the entire country had been buzzing about. "What's the Colca?" she asked.

"It's a river in the Andes. Class five and six rapids. Did you say your father robbed the Federal Reserve?"

"Not exactly. He stole the bullion while it was on its way there. Why were you kayaking in South America?"

"I run an adventure tour company."

"A *tour* company? I thought you were a cowboy."

"I own On the Edge Tours. There are brochures in the Jeep." He dropped the rag he'd been using to wipe his hands and caught her by the shoulders. "Is this why you're on the run, Lydia? Are you wanted for robbery?"

Now she almost regretted her decision to tell him. She had been regarded as the key to the missing gold for so long, it was refreshing to meet someone who didn't know, who might actually see her for who she was, not for what he could get from her.

Still, she'd come this far, she might as well finish. He would learn the truth as soon as he picked up a newspaper or turned on a television. "No, I had nothing to do with it. I've never broken the law in my life."

Derek's grip on her shoulders firmed. "I don't understand."

"Twenty-four years ago, my father hijacked a shipment of gold bullion that was on its way from a refinery in Albuquerque to the Federal Bank in Denver. Apparently, he headed for Arizona instead of Colorado. The truck was found wrecked in a gully north of Flagstaff, but it was empty. No one ever found the gold or my father."

Derek stared at her, those marvelous lake-blue eyes swirling with shadows. "You're kidding me, right?"

"I wish I was, but I assure you I've told you the complete truth."

"Damn, this is incredible."

"It was to me, too. I had no idea who my father was or what he had done until after he had died, but everyone seems to think I know where he hid the gold."

"Do you?"

"No."

"How much gold was there?"

"The refinery had poured the gold into ten-kilogram bars. There were twelve hundred of them."

"Twelve *hundred?*"

"Yes. That's twelve metric tons. At today's prices, the whole load would be worth over 170 million dollars."

He regarded her for a full minute before he released her and stepped back. He raked his fingers through his hair, then rubbed the back of his neck and squinted at her. "What was your father's name again?"

"I knew him as Zachary Smith, but his real name was Dorland."

"Zachary," he repeated. "Are you talking about Zack's gold?"

"So you did hear about it!"

He shook his head. "I remember that term from when I was a kid in Vegas. Everyone was talking about Zack's lost gold. Lots of people were heading for Arizona with picks and shovels, looking for this fortune."

"Yes. Apparently it caused quite a sensation when it happened. I understand the price of gold then was almost double what it is now."

"I thought it was a legend."

"It would have been, until my father's death stirred everything up again. Now it's been all over the news for four weeks straight and the treasure hunters are back with a vengeance, only most of them are concentrating on me instead of Arizona."

"This is unbelievable."

"I realize this must sound fantastic, but I can prove that I'm telling the truth." She turned and climbed back into the Jeep. Hooking Derek's jacket on the corner of his headrest, she knelt backward on her seat so she could reach behind it. Her gym bag lay in the back seat beside a battered leather duffel bag and a large backpack that still bore an airline baggage tag, which supported his claim that he'd just returned from Peru.

Derek's shadow fell through the angle of the open door. He spoke from behind her. "What are you doing?"

"I've got newspaper clippings," she said. Rather than struggling to pull the gym bag over the seat, she leaned over and unzipped it where it lay. A jumble of colorful lingerie puffed out of the opening. She felt her cheeks heat as she shoved the lingerie back inside and groped for the envelope she'd crammed at the bottom. "It's all here in black and white," she said, withdrawing a thick manila envelope. "You're welcome to check it out." She twisted on her knees to hold it out to him.

She hadn't realized how close he'd moved. With one hand braced on the roof and the other on the side of the door frame, his face was only inches from hers. He wasn't looking at the envelope she offered, he was looking at her.

She sat back on her heels, her pulse skipping. She wasn't used to scrutiny from handsome men. Well, not until a month ago. Since then everyone scrutinized her. "*Time* did a cover story on the bullion robbery," she said. "It's the most comprehensive summary. There's also a lot of information in a series that ran in *USA TODAY.* The pieces that ran in some of the smaller papers duplicate most of it, but they contain details the others don't."

"Why did you save them? Are you looking for the gold yourself?"

She flicked her nails against the envelope. "I'm not looking for the gold. The thought of it makes me sick to my stomach, and I want nothing to do with it. I saved these because they're about my father. I spent my entire life with him and I'm only starting to find out who he was."

"That must be rough."

"Rough? Everyone wants answers from me about him that I don't have. Over the past four weeks, I've been grilled by every law enforcement agency in the country. The house where I grew up has been searched eight times. There were so many reporters camped out around it that I had to resort to living in the basement so they wouldn't keep snapping pictures whenever I moved near a window."

He continued to watch her, his gaze softening with sympathy.

"The amateurs were the worst," she said. "I had to close the bookstore that I ran after some genius put out the rumor that Dad hid a map to the gold in one of the books. Not only did I lose the entire inventory when the place got trashed, the mob of people who couldn't get inside caused a riot that destroyed half the block."

"Geez…"

"In the space of a month, I lost my father, my home and my business. I suppose the real reason I'm on the run is because I have nothing left to go back to."

Derek took his hand from the roof and stroked his knuckles along her cheek.

Lydia was mortified to realize that she was crying. She tipped up her glasses to pinch the bridge of her nose, trying to stem the tears.

She couldn't fall apart now. She still barely knew this man. "Please, excuse me," she murmured, moving her head away from his touch. She repositioned her glasses and lifted her hand to tuck her hair behind her ear. "You've been so kind, I shouldn't be burdening you with more of my problems. I'm not at my best today…."

Her words trailed off. Her fingertips brushed only one thin lock of hair before they met a series of short tufts at the side of her head.

She dropped the envelope of clippings to the floor and ran her hands over her hair. How could she have forgotten? She leaned across the gearshift in order to see her reflection in the rearview mirror. That man with the knife, Ralph, had sliced off a wide swath from her ear to her crown. She looked absurd, like a half-shorn sheep.

Her hands began to tremble. Until now, she'd been able to hold the horror at bay, but seeing the evidence of what had been done to her—and knowing what else could have been done to her—broke through the last of her control.

She closed her eyes, but the tears wouldn't stop. There was no way to take refuge behind words this time. The loss she felt was more than physical. It was like the gut-deep hollowness she'd experienced when she'd seen the corner chiseled from her father's head-stone.

Her old life really was gone. Nothing was the same, not even her. Sobbing to catch her breath, she scrambled the rest of the way over the gearshift, opened the driver's door and tumbled out of the Jeep.

"Hey." Derek rounded the hood. "Lydia."

She held up her palm and walked toward the stream. "Give me a minute, please."

He jogged after her. "It's not that bad," he said, falling into step beside her. "It'll grow back."

She halted and turned to face him. Her humiliation deepened as she saw the compassion in his eyes. All this time, she'd been thinking about how handsome he was, but he'd probably been doing his best not to laugh at her. She looked like a clown. "This really is ridiculous. I'm not a vain woman, and I'm quite embarrassed to be this upset about my hair."

"That's not what's upsetting you."

"No?" She splayed her fingers and raked both hands up the side of her head. Her right hand tangled in a thick mass of long hair, her left skimmed quickly along her scalp. "Look at this! Don't you see it?"

"Yeah, but you're not crying over that, you're crying about everything else."

"What?"

"From the sound of it, you've been through a month of hell, but you probably held yourself together just like you did last night."

"Oh, of course. Along with all your martial-arts moves and your driving skills, you're also an expert on the psychology of women."

He snorted. "Nah, they're way too dangerous. Give me a set of Class five rapids any day."

"I'm sorry. I shouldn't have snapped at you. You were only trying to be nice."

"Will you quit apologizing?" He put his index finger under her chin. "None of this is your fault."

"Yes, it is!"

"Lydia—"

"You were right about one thing. It's not only my hair that's bothering me, it's everything else that's happened to me. But I didn't dare cry before or someone would have taken a picture or picked up the sound of my sobs with a parabolic microphone. There were people who regularly went through my garbage so even my used tissues wouldn't have been private."

Derek stroked his thumbs along her cheeks, clearing away her tears. "Gold can make people do crazy things."

"It can. It does. I wish it would all just go away and things could go back to how they used to be but they won't, Derek, because all those things were lies."

"Lydia…"

"It *is* my fault. I should have realized that my father was hiding something. The signs are obvious now, but I was so busy managing the store and taking care of him that I never suspected how he had duped everyone."

"You couldn't have known."

"I thought running away was the answer, but I've only succeeded in making things worse. I don't want to go back, but I can't go forward because my car's wrecked, the money I'd planned to live on is gone, and to top it all off there's this," she said, waving at her hair.

"Honest, it isn't that bad."

"I look like a half-clipped poodle."

"It shows off your ear. It's a pretty ear."

"You're only trying to be nice."

Instead of arguing further, Derek leaned down and settled his mouth over hers.

At first, it was shock that kept her from moving. The kiss was so unexpected, it took her a second to switch gears. Still, she could have easily pulled away.

She didn't. For the first time in days—weeks—she felt something almost...normal.

And for the first time in far too long, someone was giving instead of wanting to take.

She inhaled unsteadily through her nose, focusing on the kiss rather than her troubles. This was all right, it was just a kiss. It was pleasant and casual, as easygoing as everything else about this man.

At least, that was how it started.

Derek slid his hand along her cheek, pinched the arm of her glasses and lifted them off her nose. Cupping the back of her head in his other hand, he angled his mouth more firmly over hers and touched his tongue to her lower lip.

He tasted even better than he smelled, Lydia discovered, swaying into the kiss. Her skin tingled from the soft rasp of his beard stubble. Her entire body was warming, as if she were awakening from a long sleep.

How long had it been since she'd been kissed? She

couldn't count the last one from Benjamin. She'd known that one hadn't been real, in spite of the ring. And none of Benji's kisses had made her feel like this.

Maybe it was because of the surroundings. She could hear the chuckle of the stream beside her and the whisper of the wind in the evergreens, as fresh and wild as the sensations that hummed through her nerves. Or it could have been a leftover effect of the stress from the previous night, giving an extra boost to her heartbeat.

But more likely it was Derek. She parted her lips, sighing in pleasure as he responded with a slow caress. She'd never kissed a man like Derek Stone before. She'd already acknowledged to herself that she found him attractive, yet that wasn't the main reason she was still standing here, kissing him.

She was kissing him because she *could.*

The thought sent an extra bump to her pulse. The old Lydia, the one who had defined her life with safety and respectability, wouldn't have been caught dead kissing a man she'd known for less than half a day. It wasn't sensible or safe. This kind of behavior was as foreign to her character as…

As hijacking a truckload of gold?

God help her. There might be more of her father in her than she'd thought.

Lydia grasped Derek's waist, stepping close enough to brush her breasts against his chest. She felt him suck in his breath at the contact, his body tightening. He smoothed his hand down her back, widened his stance and pulled her flush against him.

The desire that swept through her was jarring. It was too new, too intimate to call merely pleasant anymore. She broke off the kiss on a gasp.

Derek lifted his head. He looked dazed, as if he were

as surprised by what had happened between them as she, but his expression quickly shuttered. He regarded her in silence, a muscle in his jaw twitching.

She withdrew her hands from his waist and pressed her fingertips to her mouth.

"Lydia, I'm sorry," he said. "I didn't mean to do that."

"Why did you?"

"Damned if I know."

She suspected he'd done it out of pity, but this was one instance in which she wasn't sure whether or not she wanted to know the truth. There were only so many blows her pride could take. She backed away and crossed her arms, rubbing her palms over the sleeves of her sweatshirt.

"Lydia…"

"It was an effective way to change the subject. Do you employ that strategy often?"

He walked to the edge of the stream, squatted and plunged his hands into the water. He splashed some on his face and shook his head. "That would depend on who's talking." Wiping his face on his sleeve, he looked at her over his shoulder. "It wouldn't have gone over too well with the group of men I took down the Colca."

"I shouldn't have been complaining, anyway. My problems aren't your concern."

"You're wrong, Lydia. Your problems became mine the minute I decided to stop my Jeep."

"But—"

"It's a good thing that you told me the truth. Now I have a better idea of what we're up against." He straightened, glanced around the clearing and withdrew her glasses from his pocket. He returned and held them out to her. "Those guys who attacked you last night definitely won't be giving up. Not with 170 million at stake."

At the reminder, the warmth that lingered from his kiss began to fade. She took her glasses from his palm and fitted them back on her nose. She had far more immediate problems to worry about than some meaningless kiss.

And it had to be meaningless. Men who looked like Derek Stone likely thought nothing of kissing a woman at the drop of a Stetson, and she doubted whether he received many complaints. She would take her cue from him and concentrate on their priorities. "I'm afraid you're right."

"Now that it's daylight, they could come back to follow us with a four-wheel drive." He walked to the Jeep and got behind the wheel. "We need to get out of here, Lydia," he called through the open door.

She resisted the impulse to touch her hair and moved toward him with as much dignity as she could muster. "I don't know where to go. I didn't really have a destination when I set out. I just wanted to get away from where I was."

He tried the engine. It turned over sluggishly a few times before it caught. "I've got a place a few miles outside Durango that's as private as you could get," he said as he hopped back out. He slammed the hood closed and motioned for her to get in the passenger side. "You're welcome to stay with me for a few days until the heat dies down. I guarantee no one would look for you there."

"I couldn't possibly…"

"Why not? Do you have a better idea?"

Since she didn't, she remained silent.

"The invitation's got nothing to do with our kiss, if

that's what you're worried about," he said. "I'm not expecting to pick up where we left off."

She tried for a casual shrug, in spite of the tickle of excitement that followed his words. She wasn't sure she would object if they did pick up where they had left off. Would his lips feel as good the second time?

He walked to her door, swung it all the way open and braced the heel of his hand against the edge. "I hate to rush you again, Lydia, but we have to get moving."

She forced her mind to the matter at hand. This was no time to be concerned with proprieties. Derek's offer was not only generous, it was sensible. After all, she didn't have a car and had little money, so even if she knew where to go, she'd have no way to get there. Staying with him was her best option, at least until she figured out where else to go.

And darn it, she *wanted* to go with him.

Without further delay, she climbed into the Jeep.

The tread of heavy boots on concrete echoed from the corridor. Hart McAllister grasped the edge of his desk to lever himself out of his chair, gripped his cane and moved to the center of the room. By the time the three men were escorted through the door, Hart had assumed a position in front of the flag.

He was well aware of the impact of his appearance, and he cultivated it to his full advantage. His uniform was spotless, his medals sparkling in the harsh light that came from the bare bulbs in the ceiling. His hair was a thick mane of dignified silver, his chiseled features were honed as leanly as his sixty-year-old body. With the backdrop of the Stars and Stripes providing the reminder of patriotism and the cane lending him the dignity of a wounded hero, he could deliver a message before he opened his mouth.

Hart took his time lifting his hand from his cane to return the men's salutes. They expected it of him. He was a leader. And leaders led.

He nodded to the sentry by the doorway. "Leave us."

"Yes, Colonel."

The sound of the latching door echoed starkly from the cinder block walls. Aside from the flag, the desk and the army cot behind it, the room was as bare as cell, but the men expected that of him, too. Comfort wasn't a concern for a soldier. These new headquarters were superbly defensible, a lucky find after the Canyon Brotherhood had been forced to relocate. It was the perfect location from which to launch their final campaign. "Private Brown."

Earl shifted from one foot to the other. His training in military protocol wasn't as ingrained as that of his companions, since his term of service had been the shortest. He'd washed out of the National Guard after a jealous superior had ambushed him with a psych assessment. "Yes, sir?"

"Explain to me why you're here."

"The woman took off. We had to do something."

"You were told to watch her and wait. You were also told not to harm her until she talked."

"We didn't." Earl glanced at Ralph. "Nothing permanent, anyway."

"Private Henry?" Hart asked, shifting his regard to Ralph. Ralph Henry was an ex-marine. He'd come to the Canyon Brotherhood after he'd been found guilty of torturing prisoners in his care. The charges had been completely unjustified—like so many soldiers, he'd been made a scapegoat by the politicians for doing his duty.

"She had help," Ralph said. "Some cowboy showed up before we could get her in the van and took us by surprise. We lost them when they turned off the road."

Hart had already heard the details from his subordinates when the men had reported in, so he'd had time to prepare himself for the disappointment. Still, this team was one of his best when it came to getting results. Their leader, Pete Wilcox, had been a Green Beret. He'd been trained in unconventional warfare and was accustomed to operating independently in enemy territory. Yet the Army had viewed his zeal as insubordination and had repaid his loyalty with a dishonorable discharge. After years of service, Pete had been cast adrift with no reward other than a stained record and a simmering resentment for the government.

Love of country, coupled with hate for the authorities. The men who joined the Canyon Brotherhood had both. All were patriots like Hart, men who had served honorably only to watch their lives fall apart when the government they had fought for abandoned them. They shared a common dream of someday evening the score. To be on the winning side, to show the world they were still warriors to be reckoned with.

It was a dream that had given Hart focus and had made him powerful. Under his direction, the Brotherhood had amassed a fortune. He'd had no scruples about its source—like every leader in history, he understood that the end justified the means.

"What will you need to find them, Sergeant Wilcox?" Hart asked, moving his gaze to Pete.

Pete scowled. "We'll need more firepower, for one thing. A better vehicle, too."

"I'll alert the armory. You're authorized to sign out what you need from the stores."

"Are you sending us back out?" Earl asked, an eager gleam in his eyes at the prospect of action.

Hart clenched his fingers around the curved handle of his cane. "The Brotherhood doesn't give up. Adversity merely strengthens the true fighter."

"You can count on us, sir," Ralph said, rubbing the bruise on his jaw. "The Brotherhood ain't gonna walk away from that gold."

Hart waited until the men had filed out, then limped back to his desk and eased into his chair. Rather than returning his attention to the manifesto he'd been working on when the men had arrived, he slid open the top drawer. For a moment, he gazed at the newspaper clipping that rested within, then picked it up carefully and smoothed his fingertips over the photograph.

The article was only a month old, yet he'd touched it so many times, the paper was becoming worn. It had been twenty-four years since he'd seen that face. The hair was different, but he would recognize those features even if he were ninety. It belonged to the past, to the time before the Brotherhood, when Hart had had a different dream.

Walk away from the gold? Not while he still breathed. He'd done that once before, and nothing, not even the Brotherhood, was going to keep Hart McAllister from reclaiming what was rightfully his.

Chapter 3

"Is that your house?" Lydia asked.

Derek brought the Jeep to a stop at the foot of the drive so that Lydia could get a look at the place before they started winding their way through the trees. "That's it."

"The way it blends into the surroundings is lovely. It looks as if it was built right into the side of the cliff."

"It was."

"You must have a tremendous view from up there." She flattened one hand on the dashboard and leaned forward, her lips parting in fascination.

He was hard-pressed not to do the same himself, only he was looking at Lydia, not his house. The sunset was tinting her face bronze, putting a healthy glow into her pale cheeks. She had tried to minimize the effects of her chopped hair by smoothing what was left of it into a tight bun, but it made the difference in the lengths more noticeable. While her longer hair was stretched straight, the short chunks had rebounded into soft, chestnut curls.

She was as resilient as her hair. He'd half expected her to withdraw from him after her emotional storm this morning, but her initial awkwardness when they'd started out had gradually thawed. She was too warm-hearted by nature to remain aloof for long. In fact, during the trip here—made slower by the necessity of sticking to back roads to avoid possible pursuit—their conversation had progressed to the point of tentative friendship.

He knew he should be pleased, since his strategy was working out exactly as he had hoped. This was what he was good at. His psych training, combined with his gift for following the right hunches, had made him one of the FBI's top profilers. His reputation for extracting information from a suspect had been legendary.

Not that he regarded Lydia as a suspect, but she was the key to finding Zack's gold. And the gold was the bait he needed to draw out the Colonel, the elusive leader of the Canyon Brotherhood.

The group's crimes included theft, extortion and drug pushing, to name a few. No capital offenses, nothing to kick them to the top of a Most Wanted list, but there was a pattern to the crimes that was more alarming than the crimes themselves. The Brotherhood was too focused and too fanatic to be a simple criminal gang. Derek was certain they had a hidden agenda. They had to be stopped, and with Lydia's help, he planned to make sure they were.

So why did he feel like a piece of crud?

The answer to that was easy. He liked Lydia. Her restrictive upbringing and her limited experience might have left her naive, but she was an intelligent, spirited woman. After everything she'd gone through, she could use a real friend. The deeper he got into this, the less comfortable he became with the strategy he was using. Sure, it had worked in his FBI days, but there had been plenty of things he'd done back then that he wouldn't do now.

Yet now that he'd started, it was too late to alter course. He still needed information from Lydia, and she still needed protection. This was the surest way to accomplish both objectives. Nothing had changed.

Except for the fact that he'd kissed her.

He knew he shouldn't have done it. Winning her trust and being her friend was one thing, but he'd crossed the line with that kiss. He hadn't been thinking about the gold or the Brotherhood or what would happen if he failed this task. No, he hadn't been thinking at all.

It had caught him by surprise. Who would have guessed a woman like Lydia could kiss like that? Half-innocent, half-wild, and sexy enough to make him hard just remembering the feel of her mouth. It was a complication he didn't need.

Damn.

"How on earth does it stay up?" she asked.

He reined in his thoughts. She was talking about the house, not him.

He moved his gaze to the glass-and-redwood building that appeared to be suspended over the gully in front of them. The windows that wrapped across the front of both stories blazed with reflected sunset, all but obscuring the pillars that supported it. "Impressive, isn't it?"

"It's magnificent. It looks as if it's floating on air."

"See those long, thin shadows?" he asked, pointing to the bottom of the structure.

"I think so."

"Each one is a support pillar built around a tungsten rod that's sunk thirty feet into the cliff face. There's also a suspension-bridge-strength cable that runs through the floor of the second story and is bolted into more rods on the top of the bluff."

"Well, that's a relief. It looks quite disconcerting the way it's positioned on the edge... Oh, now I get it."

"Get what?"

"The name of your tour company. Was 'On the Edge' inspired by that house?"

"Partly. It's also because of the kind of tours that I run."

She nodded. Derek had seen her studying one of his brochures earlier—he wasn't sure whether she'd been verifying his story or had simply been curious—yet whatever her motives, seeing the brochures had definitely strengthened the trust that she was developing. "Like white-water kayaking, rock climbing and survival treks," she said.

"Right. On the Edge specializes in high-risk packages. This is my home base, but I have customers all over the country. They often suggest the destination. My job is to scout it out, deal with the red tape and logistics and then make sure they get back alive."

"You sound very proud of what you do. You must enjoy your work."

"It suits me. Besides, people pay good money to be scared spitless."

"No offense, Derek, but I can't imagine doing that."

"My clients do it for the rush. Facing danger and overcoming it triggers a high all its own. You got a taste of it yourself yesterday."

Lydia poked at her glasses and glanced at him speculatively.

"What?" he asked.

"That explains the look," she said. "After you knocked out those men, you seemed...pleased."

He was surprised she had noticed. "Ambushing three guys in the dark wasn't that much of a challenge, but it did give me a good workout."

"Is that why you came back to help me? Because of the thrill?"

"Nah, I'm just a nice guy."

She smiled. It was the first full one she'd given him, and for a second he couldn't think. Her eyes sparkled, her cheeks dimpled and her lips stretched into a pixie grin that made his pulse thud in response.

Oh, hell. He wanted to kiss her again.

He eased the Jeep forward to start up the winding driveway. "You said you ran a bookstore, right?"

"Yes. It's awfully tame compared to what you do, but I've always loved to read. There are plenty of thrills in books, too." She craned her neck to keep the house in sight as long as she could, then fell back into her seat with a sigh. "But I must admit I've never come across anything like that house. Did you design it yourself?"

"I can't take credit for that. The man who had it built was more interested in privacy than in adrenaline rushes. He wanted a place where no one could sneak up on him."

"Well, he certainly accomplished that goal. Was he a celebrity? I've heard that plenty of Hollywood actors have private homes around Aspen and Vail."

"Tony Monaco's not a celebrity, but he's very wealthy. He loaned me the start-up capital for my tour company. I house-sit this place for him as part of the package."

"That sounds like a good deal."

"Yeah," he drawled. "Tony's all heart."

"Does he use this house often?"

"I've been here seven years and he's only stayed here twice. He has places all over the world."

"I can't imagine wealth like that."

"Neither can I. It makes 170 million look like pocket change."

She rubbed her palms over her sleeves. "I suppose he wanted privacy for the same reason I do. People must be after him all the time."

"You could say that. See that glint in the rocks to the left?" he asked, slowing as he neared the final turn.

"Yes. What is it?"

"A motion detector. We've passed a dozen of them. The property's full of automated sensors that are monitored by a computer. Tony's security system is state of the art."

"I can understand why you said this would be a good place for me to stay," she said as the gates that blocked the drive came into view. "All you need is a moat, and you'd have a castle."

Derek pulled up beside a square, brick post. He opened his window and stretched his arm to reach the keypad on the post's side. "No one's going to bother you here, Lydia. I guarantee you'll be safe."

"Thank you, Derek." She sighed. "I must have said that a dozen times by now. I'm so glad you happened to be driving past when I needed help."

Derek's conscience twanged. He tamped it down and punched in the code to open the gates. "Well, you can stop thanking me. I'm not helping you just because I'm a nice guy."

"Oh?"

"I'm doing this to pay off a debt."

She pressed into the passenger door. "What?"

"Relax, I don't mean that I'm expecting to get a piece of that gold everyone wants from you. It's because I know what it's like to be in trouble and on the run."

"Why? What happened?"

"It's a long story, but what it boils down to is someone helped me once. By helping you, I'm evening the score."

And that, he realized, was the absolute truth.

Lydia pulled her feet onto the couch and gazed at the flames that danced on the stone hearth. It was hard to believe that less than twenty-four hours ago she had been sitting in her living room with the lights off and her bag packed, every penny from her emergency cookie jar stash zippered into her purse. She'd waited for the rain to get worse, praying she would have the nerve to move when it did. Never in her wildest dreams would she have guessed she would end up in a place like this.

Wrapping her arms around her folded legs, she laid her cheek on her knee and glanced around the spacious living room. The interior of this home was as impressive as the exterior. The upper level began on the top of the cliff in a spacious, skylit foyer with a floor of natural stone. From there, an arching corridor wound past the bedrooms to a gallery that overlooked the living area. Wide, pine planking formed the floor in the lower section, softened by scattered carpets with Navaho-style geometric designs. The furniture that was grouped in front of the granite fireplace was big, masculine and comfortable, upholstered in mellow earth tones of sienna and rust.

The view of the fading sunset that stretched beyond the front windows was so breathtaking, it had taken Lydia a good five minutes to notice that a Picasso hung on the wall opposite the fireplace.

There were two Modigliani nudes in the guest bedroom Derek had shown her to. Like the Picasso, the paintings were sensuously vibrant, and they somehow managed to complement the Southwestern decorating theme of the house. The same mixture of the elegant and the rustic extended to the bathroom that adjoined her bedroom: the tub was an old-fashioned claw-foot design, yet its faucets were made from turquoise and silver.

The scope of Tony Monaco's wealth was difficult for Lydia to grasp—this house alone must have cost a fortune. Was this the kind of thing her father had hoped to attain when he had stolen that bullion? If it was, he must have hated the modest home in Denver that she'd tended so carefully.

"I've locked up and activated the alarm," Derek said. "Better not wander outside or you'll set it off."

She lifted her head to watch him as he came down the stairs from the gallery. His hair was damp from his shower and slicked back against his head, and his jaw was smooth from a fresh shave. He'd changed into a clean pair of well broken-in blue jeans and a cream-colored golf shirt. And he looked so handsome, she found it hard not to stare. "I wasn't planning to go out," she said.

"I doubt if anyone could have followed us, but I do get the odd bear nosing around." He crossed the floor to a low wooden shelf that was built into the wall beneath the window and squatted to look through it. "Did you find everything you need?"

"Yes, thanks." She unfolded her legs and smoothed the fabric of her jogging pants. Besides her underwear, this was one of only two sets of spare clothing she'd brought with her—she'd been more concerned about taking the important items, like her papers and the clippings she'd collected. She'd planned to purchase what she needed once she was safely on her way. Twenty-four hours ago, she'd thought the beige jogging suit was a sensible choice, since it was warm, comfortable and didn't need ironing, but now she wished she hadn't chosen something quite so, well, dowdy.

Derek straightened up with an object that looked like a remote control unit in his hand. He pointed it at the windows. An instant later, the orange-streaked darkness beyond the glass dissolved into a shimmer of gray.

"What happened?" Lydia asked.

"The glass in these windows has a charged layer that can turn opaque."

"Oh, my. I've read about that but I've never actually seen it."

"It's a security measure to keep the light inside at night." He shrugged. "I think a set of blinds would work just as well, but Tony likes his gadgets." He aimed the remote at a large, pine cabinet that was set against the back wall.

She turned her head just in time to see the doors of the cabinet swing open to reveal a large-screen television.

"It would be a good idea to check out the news so we can see if there's anything about you," Derek said. He moved to a chair that faced the TV and sat on the arm. "You don't mind, do you?"

She twisted sideways on the couch so she could see the screen. He'd tuned it to CNN. Inwardly, she cringed, remembering the flurry of stories that had followed her father's death. "Of course, I don't mind," she said. "It's a sensible suggestion."

Images of soldiers in the Middle East flickered across the screen behind the anchorwoman, followed by a report of a flood in China. Lydia watched in silence as several more news items were given the usual CNN treatment of terse sound bites and video clips.

"I don't get newspaper delivery up here," Derek said as the news turned to politics. "But we can download the online editions and check those out, too."

"My father used to go through four newspapers every morning before he left the house," Lydia said. "I didn't realize until later that he had been checking for news about himself. I hope I won't need to spend the rest of my life doing that, too."

"It sounds as if he knew how to stay out of sight."

"He did. He was preoccupied by safety, which is likely why I turned out that way, too. He used to get upset if I forgot to lock the door or was two minutes late getting home from the bookstore."

"Did you always live with your father?"

His question stirred a trace of old resentment. Lydia pushed it aside—that part of her life was over, too. "Not always. When I turned twenty-one I moved into an apartment of my own, but I moved back home after my dad had his first heart attack. I worried about him being alone."

"You were a good daughter."

"I loved him. We got along well. It was a complete shock to learn he'd been lying to me."

"Sometimes people lie because they feel they have no choice," he said quietly. "Maybe your father believed he was keeping the truth from you for your own good."

"If he'd told me the truth, none of this would be happening. It's my fault, you know."

"What is?"

"My dad hated getting his picture taken. I'd always assumed it was because he was shy and because his pictures turned out as horribly as mine did."

Derek muted the sound and looked at her. "How's that?"

"I'm not photogenic." She smiled wryly. "Not that I would expect to be, but that's beside the point. If I had known the real reason my dad avoided photographs, I wouldn't have let the *Nugget* publish his picture. You see, our bookstore won an award from the chamber of commerce, and I wanted to make sure he got the proper credit for our success. I thought I was doing him a favor to have his picture published with mine."

"What happened?"

"It seems his appearance hadn't changed all that much in twenty-four years. Evidently, someone saw that picture and recognized him from the photographs that had been circulated at the time of the gold robbery. The week after the article ran, he was attacked, probably by the same men who attacked me." She took a deep breath before she could go on. "They tried to beat the secret of where he left the gold out of him, but he didn't tell them anything. His heart gave out and they left him for dead, but he lived long enough to confess his real name and what had happened to the policemen who found him."

"Geez." Derek left his chair and came to sit beside her on the couch, his back to the TV screen. "It wasn't your fault."

She held up her palm. "Don't worry, I'm not going to break down again."

He touched his index finger to her leg. "No one could blame you if you do. You've had a lot to deal with, and I get the feeling that you've had to do it alone, in spite of the crowd that was around you."

His insight brought a lump to her throat. "Yes, well, I won't blubber about it the way I did this morning."

"You can tell me whatever you want, Lydia. After what you've gone through, you could use a friend." He squeezed her knee. "Your father must have known it would be hard to hide his identity forever."

"Maybe. I don't know. I never got the chance to ask him."

"That's why you saved those newspaper articles about him, isn't it? You need a framework so you can fill in the missing pieces."

"There are plenty of missing pieces, all right." From the corner of her vision, she caught sight of a familiar image on the TV. "Oh, no."

Derek twisted to look over his shoulder, then turned up the sound.

"In a bizarre development to a story we brought you last month," the announcer said, "Lydia Smith, the daughter of the late Zachary Dorland, has apparently vanished as mysteriously as the gold bullion her notorious father stole from the Federal Reserve twenty-four years ago."

Lydia gritted her teeth as she looked at the photograph behind the announcer. It was worse than any that had been published yet. "That's the one from my driver's licence," she murmured. "I look like a felon."

"The DMV makes everyone looks like a felon," Derek said.

The announcer continued. "Sources say Ms. Smith's wrecked car was found abandoned on a lonely stretch of road near Leadville, Colorado. The Denver police are calling her disappearance suspicious. When asked whether they believe Ms. Smith has dropped out of sight in order to retrieve her father's illicit fortune, their official reply was, 'No comment.'"

The photo of Lydia was replaced with a scene of traffic chaos on what appeared to be the main street of a town that she didn't recognize.

"However, as this footage shows," the anchorwoman said, "hundreds of hopeful treasure hunters have already converged on Leadville. The local hardware stores have reportedly sold out their stock of picks and shovels. The hunt for the legendary Zack's gold, and for the woman who has become famous across America as the Million Dollar Mouse, is turning this quiet region into—"

Derek clicked off the television and dropped the remote on the couch.

Lydia lifted her chin, striving for composure. She'd told him she wasn't going to blubber, so she wouldn't.

But did CNN have to use that nickname? She wasn't sure which tabloid had coined it, since it had caught on immediately. It was so humiliating, she felt like screaming. More than that, she felt like picking up something heavy and throwing it at the television.

Yet as always, she did neither.

"This is incredible," Derek said.

"As you said this morning, gold makes people do crazy things."

"No, I meant the way the story was treated, stuck at the end of the newscast like a novelty piece." He scowled as he looked at her. "Doesn't anyone understand the danger you're in? If they saw your car was wrecked, and they know your father had been attacked

by someone who wanted the gold, you'd think they
would be more concerned about your welfare. That
should be their top priority."

"It's been like that all along. The real crimes get lost
underneath the gold frenzy the press has whipped up."

"What I don't get is why everyone is so sure you
know where the stuff is. It's not like you were there."

"Well, actually, I was."

His scowl deepened. "How? You said you were only
a kid."

"I was five. I don't remember any of it, but according to the police and all the reports I've read about the
robbery, my father had taken me along with him in the
cab of the truck. I was there when he overpowered the
driver. It was all part of his getaway plan. He hadn't
wanted to risk being spotted when he came back to get
me. You see, my mother had died when I was an infant,
so he was a single parent and—"

"He took a child on a gold heist? Damn it, what was
he thinking? You could have been killed when that truck
crashed."

She pulled her feet onto the couch again and wrapped
her arms tightly around her legs. "He couldn't have
known the accident would happen. And he certainly
made up for his lapse in parental protectiveness afterward. He couldn't have kept me safer if he'd wrapped
me up in a cocoon."

Derek continued to study her. "Geez, this explains
it. I can see why you ran. You were a witness."

"That's what the police tell me. They claimed that I
wasn't too young, that I should remember something,
but I don't."

"The police wouldn't be the only ones who believe
that. As long as the gold is out there and the media

keeps the story alive, you'll be the target of every nut-bar who can heft a shovel."

"I know. I don't want to spend the rest of my life hiding, but maybe I'll have to."

Derek leaned closer. Settling his hands on her shoulders, he looked into her eyes. "That bullion is at the root of all your troubles."

"I don't deny that."

"Seems to me instead of running from it, you might want to think about finding it yourself."

She let go of her legs and pushed herself backward, sliding across the couch cushion to break free of his hold. "That gold cost my father his life and ruined mine. I don't want anything to do with it."

"Then give it back to the feds, or give it to charity. Once everyone knows it's been found, no one would have any reason to bother you. All the craziness should stop."

"That sounds fine in theory, except I don't know where it is. I told you that already."

"Are you sure you don't?"

"Do you think I'm *lying?*"

"Whoa, don't get mad at me. I only meant you might know something and not realize it, like the way you hadn't realized the real reason your father was camera shy." Derek retrieved the remote and focused on the buttons, then aimed it toward the cabinet with the TV. Strains of classical music floated through the air. He jabbed another button and the music switched to country. "You want some dinner?" he asked, tipping his head toward the far end of the living room where the kitchen began. "I grill a mean steak."

Lydia dropped her face in her hands. "I'm sorry for snapping at you again. I understand that you're only trying to help."

"Hey, forget it. I shouldn't have butted in. There's nothing wrong with holing up somewhere and staying out of sight, just like you're doing here," he said. "The heat's bound to die down eventually."

Holing up, Lydia repeated to herself. Like a scared little mouse, or like a spinster daughter spending her youth with her reclusive father and living her life through her books.

The Million Dollar Mouse. The reason the nickname hurt so much was because it carried too much truth.

She lifted her head. "Derek, you told me you were in trouble and on the run once, too."

"That's right."

"How did you solve it?"

He played with the remote some more, changing the color of the windows from gray to indigo. "I had help."

"It was Tony Monaco who helped you, wasn't it?"

"I guess that wasn't hard to figure out."

"What kind of trouble were you in?"

He rose to his feet and went over to the fireplace to add another log. "It wasn't like your trouble, Lydia. All my problems, I brought on myself."

"If you'd rather not talk about it…"

"No, it's only fair." Propping his elbow on the mantel, he shifted his weight to one leg and crossed his feet at the ankles. "You trusted me enough to level with me, so I owe you the truth, too."

Though his pose was relaxed, she could sense he wasn't as casual as he seemed. Yet he was right about one thing. So far, she'd been the one doing most of the talking. It was only fair if she learned more about him.

"I used to gamble," he said. "Poker mostly. I was good at cards, but I didn't do it for the money, I did it for the rush."

A gambler? She could see that. It would go along with Derek's whole on-the-edge lifestyle.

"When I started to lose, instead of admitting I had a problem and trying to get help, I got mixed up with a loan shark."

Lydia felt a chill, in spite of the warmth that was radiating from the fire. "I've never met a loan shark, but I understand they can be extremely ruthless."

"This one was. I owed him four hundred grand on an eighty grand loan. I was ready to do whatever it took to pay him back."

"Had he threatened to kill you?"

"Not exactly." He glanced at her. "His trademark punishment for men who couldn't pay was to cut off their testicles."

"Oh, my God."

"Yeah."

"What happened?"

"Once you hear this, you might have second thoughts about staying with me."

Somehow she managed to keep her gaze on his face. Could this man be…maimed? He seemed so virile, it didn't seem possible he was lacking anything. "Whatever you tell me, Derek, I'll understand."

"Okay, here goes. Except for the gambling, I had lived the straight and narrow. I had a good job and made a decent living, but I knew I wouldn't be able to raise the kind of cash I needed honestly." He waited, as if gauging her reaction. "I decided to rob a jewelry store."

A month ago, before she'd learned that her father had been a thief, Lydia wouldn't have been able to imagine sitting calmly in the same room with a man who admitted to planning a robbery.

Yet a lot had changed since then, beginning with her

sensibilities. Not all criminals were beasts like the men who had attacked her. She'd lived her entire life with a man who had broken the law, and while she didn't like his deception, that hadn't changed her feelings for him. He'd been a good father and she'd loved him dearly. Besides, she'd discovered for herself how extreme circumstances could cause people to behave in ways they otherwise wouldn't.

Still, it was unsettling. "Did you go through with it?" she asked.

"Uh-huh, but I didn't get far." One corner of his mouth lifted into a lopsided smile, despite the grim facts he was relating. "As it turned out, choosing to rob that particular store was the luckiest break of my life. The guy who owned it turned out to be Tony Monaco."

"How was that lucky?"

"Instead of pressing charges, Tony listened to my story. He figured it wouldn't do either of us any good if I went to prison, so he bought up my markers from the loan shark and gave me a fresh start out here."

"That's…"

His smile grew. "Sounds like something from a fairy tale, doesn't it?"

"Well, you have to admit it's unusually generous of Tony."

"Yeah, but believe me, he's no fairy godfather," Derek said. "Tony doesn't run a charity. He expects to be paid back in full, and I'm doing everything in my power to make sure that I do."

A log snapped in the fireplace, shooting sparks toward the chimney. Lydia took a moment to consider what Derek had said. She knew he couldn't be just another treasure hunter, since he hadn't known who she was when he'd risked his life to rescue her. Furthermore, he hadn't known she'd witnessed the gold robbery until a few minutes ago. And yet…

She cleared her throat. "No offense, Derek, but it seems to me that you must realize 170 million in gold bullion would go a long way to paying off a debt."

His smile disappeared. He was silent for a while, as if debating with himself whether or not to go on. When he finally spoke, his tone had hardened. "I can understand why you would suspect that, Lydia. I just admitted I was a thief."

"Derek—"

"But Tony wouldn't accept the gold as payment, even if it was twice that amount. He's got strong opinions about justice. The gold was stolen, and one of the conditions of Tony's loan is that I have to stay on the right side of the law. There aren't any shortcuts. I have to earn my way out of Tony's debt."

"He sounds like an…unusual man."

"He's one of a kind." He pushed away from the mantel. "And for what it's worth, I swear to you right now on all the honor I have left, I don't want any of your father's gold for myself."

This was the second time he'd said as much, yet the sincerity in his voice now was unmistakable. So was the flash of emotion in his eyes when he spoke about his honor. It was obvious to Lydia that his brief foray into crime still haunted him, in spite of the extenuating circumstances that had led to it.

That eased her doubts more than his words could have.

"I owe Tony more than money," he said. "It was because of him that I kicked my gambling habit—I haven't so much as bought a lottery ticket in seven years. Now I get my rushes from the tours I run."

Although Lydia was curious to learn more about the eccentric Tony Monaco, she was more interested in what Derek was revealing about himself. "I'm glad you told me about this, Derek. The way you worked things out is inspiring. You not only solved your problems, you changed your life for the better."

"Yeah." He shoved his hands into his pockets. "And thanks to Tony, I can still sing baritone."

She tried to keep her gaze on his face, yet she couldn't help glancing downward to the region in question. Her cheeks heated. "Well, that certainly puts what was done to my hair in perspective."

Chapter 4

Lydia draped a bath towel around her shoulders, picked up the scissors and studied her reflection in the bathroom mirror. As far back as she could remember, she'd had long hair. When she'd been younger, she'd gathered it into pigtails or a ponytail at the back of her head. She didn't know when she had started twisting it into a bun. Perhaps she'd seen a magazine picture of a model and had secretly hoped to look as striking herself.

Of course, the style would work for a tall, svelte blonde who had been gifted with cheekbones that could slice bread, but it had never been flattering for Lydia. With nothing to soften her pointed chin and her large eyes, wearing her hair in a bun did tend to emphasize her resemblance to a rodent.

The style was sensible, though. It took practically no time to fix her hair in the morning before she went to

work. In a way, it was safer, too, because by scraping
her hair into a sexless bun, she avoided the disappointment of striving for more than she should. She had re-
signed herself to the fact that she shouldn't waste her
efforts trying to improve her appearance. As her father
had always assured her, looks weren't important.

Would Derek have kissed her last night instead of de-
frosting two steaks if she'd been a tall, svelte blonde?

Lydia made a face at the mirror. Her decision to trim
her hair had nothing to do with Derek, it was for herself. Trivial or not, it was another step in her decision
to start a new life. And she couldn't very well look any
worse, could she? Before she could lose her nerve,
Lydia grabbed a lock of wet hair, held it out to the side
and snipped it three inches from her scalp. It fell to the
bathroom floor with a sigh, as if relieved to be finally
gone.

She blew out her breath, surprised how good that had
felt, so she grasped another lock and repeated the pro-
cess. The pile at her feet grew as she worked her way
around her head, the scissors flashing with reckless finality.

It got easier the more she did—she already knew the
principles of cutting hair. She'd given haircuts to her father for years, because he'd hated to go to barbers. He'd
claimed the barber chairs hurt his back. Of course, that
had likely been a lie, too. But she'd loved him, so she
hadn't considered doubting him.

She lowered the scissors and regarded her reflection
critically. She could still see a trace of the swath above
her left ear that had been shorn by Ralph's knife, but
it wasn't as noticeable as it had been. With a little lay-
ering, it would practically disappear. Encouraged, she
sifted her fingers through her hair, held her hand at an

angle and trimmed the ends above her knuckles. Taking control was invigorating, even if it was only her hair.

She already looked drastically different from that horrid picture on her driver's licence. The shorter her hair got, the springier it became. The weight of it had dragged it straight, but now it was forming into curls as it dried. Not only that, there appeared to be touches of red. She fluffed her hair with her free hand, then leaned closer to the mirror and tilted her head. Sure enough, in this light, there were hints of auburn in some of the curls.

Who would have guessed her hair could look anything but plain, mousy brown? Her father's hair had been fine and poker straight. It had been completely gray by the time he'd died, but it had once been raven black. He'd had pale, blue eyes, so she'd always known she hadn't inherited her coloring from him.

An image floated into her mind, superimposing itself over her reflection in the mirror. It was a woman in a black dress, with short, curly hair that was vibrant red. Lydia could remember the way the ends had sprung back against her fingers. It was the same as what she felt as she touched her own curls.

I love you, baby. Remember that.

Mommy!

The scissors clattered to the floor. The image and the voice dissolved as quickly as they had arisen. Lydia told herself it must have been her imagination. She couldn't be remembering her mother. Rose Hobbs Smith had died when Lydia had been an infant.

Or had that been yet another one of Zachary's lies?

The possibility made her pause. Everything she had taken for granted was in question. It wasn't only her father she needed to learn the truth about. What if she had known her mother? What if her mother was still alive?

You might know something and not realize it.

Could what Derek had said be true? Lydia clutched the edge of the counter beneath the mirror and closed her eyes, trying to recapture the image of the woman's face. Nothing came. She couldn't picture what the face had looked like anymore. It had slipped out of reach, like the fragment of a dream upon waking.

A faint knocking sounded through the bedroom door. She blinked her eyes open and hurriedly brushed the stray hairs off her cheeks. "Just a minute," she called. She removed the towel from her shoulders and used it to sweep the hair on the floor into a pile, then left the bathroom and walked through the bedroom. "I'll be right there."

"Don't rush." Derek's voice came from the other side of the door. "I thought I heard the water running so I figured you were up."

"Yes, I've been awake for a while." She took off her glasses to blow off a piece of hair that had stuck to a lens. "Is something wrong?"

"No, I have to go out. I wondered if you wanted to come along."

She set her glasses back on her nose and glanced down to make sure there weren't any hairs on her jogging suit before she grasped the doorknob and pulled open the door. "Do you think that would be safe?" she asked. "What if someone sees me?"

He was standing in the corridor, one shoulder propped against the side of the door frame and his ankles crossed, looking every inch a long, lean cowboy. He straightened up slowly, his eyes widening.

She brushed her bare nape self-consciously. "Don't laugh. I had to do something."

"Why the hell would I laugh?" he asked, his voice rough.

"Never mind. Where were you going?"

"Nowhere public." He brought one hand to her cheek. His fingertips whispered across her skin as he touched one of her curls. "I always like to take my equipment out for a run when it's been idle for a while."

Her cheek warmed at his caress. "Your equipment?"

"When it's practical, I fly my tour groups on site myself."

"Do you have a plane?"

He eased the curl behind her ear and traced his thumb along the rim. "A helicopter."

"I suppose Peru wouldn't have been within helicopter range."

"You're right. I booked local transportation and suppliers when I organized that one." He rubbed her earlobe. "Do you like to fly?"

"I don't know. I've never flown."

"Never?"

"I had no reason to go anywhere. I—" Her voice hitched as he gave her earlobe a light squeeze. "If you're doing that to change the subject…"

He withdrew his hand and placed it on the door frame above her head. "Sorry. Forgot myself again."

Lydia drew in the musky, sweet tang of sandalwood that rose from the gap at the neck of his shirt and thought about how good his kiss had tasted. But as he'd already told her, that kiss had nothing to do with the reason she was here. That caress just now had probably meant no more than the kiss had. He appeared to be a person who liked to touch.

She'd never been comfortable with casual touching—she liked a wide buffer of personal space—yet she didn't mind when Derek touched her. And although he was crowding her space, standing in front of the threshold so that she wouldn't be able to squeeze past, she had no desire to step back.

The simple reason was that she liked him. The feeling had been building from the moment he'd stopped on the road to help her. But if she wanted to pinpoint the instant the balance had tipped in his favor, it would have been the evening before, when he had revealed the mistakes in his past.

It took an exceptional man to admit his weakness. There was far more to Derek Stone than simply his good looks.

On the other hand, all this rationalizing about his character could just be a convenient way to justify the fact that she was wildly attracted to him.

"You might have been right yesterday," she said.

"About what?"

"I could know more than I realize I do. Something strange happened when I was looking in the mirror a few minutes ago. I thought I remembered my mother's face, though I had been told she'd died when I was only a few months old."

"Did she look like you?"

"I've never seen her picture. My dad had claimed that all the photographs of her and the first five years of my life had been lost in a fire before we moved to Denver, which was obviously another lie. But she couldn't have looked like me."

"How do you know?"

"My dad told me. He said she was beautiful."

He slapped his free hand to the door frame beside her shoulder. "So are you, Lydia."

"That's nice of you to say, Derek, but I'm more concerned with what that memory might indicate. I think that seeing my hair short is what triggered it. And this, too," she said, twining a curl around her finger. "It's as if I remember the feel of it."

"Does that upset you?"

"It's spooky, but it's encouraging, too." She clasped her fingers under her chin, feeling the same reckless resolve as she had when she'd picked up the scissors. "I believe you're right about something else, too. My troubles aren't going to go away until that gold does. I'll always be viewed as a witness, no matter what I say."

His gaze lit with a sudden gleam. Keeping his hands on the door frame, he leaned closer. Beneath his short sleeves, the muscles in his forearms roped with tension. "Sounds like you've been doing some thinking."

Part of her couldn't believe she was considering this. The very idea of the gold bullion repulsed her, yet it was the biggest obstacle to her new life. It couldn't compare to having a loan shark after her, but like Derek, she wasn't going to solve her problem until she faced it.

She moved her hands from her chin to her mouth, pressing her knuckles to her lips. "I've already lost twenty-nine years being obsessed with safety, and I don't want to spend the rest of my life holing up somewhere like the mouse people say I am. Recovering that gold and giving it back to the government is the only logical solution to my problems."

"That's a gutsy decision."

She smiled against her knuckles. "It is, isn't it?"

"Absolutely. And it's the right one."

"I'm not sure. Actually, now that I've said it, I don't know where to start."

"The answer has to be in there someplace." He tapped his fingertip against her temple. "It's just a matter of getting it out."

"I can't very well keep cutting my hair to trigger

memories or I'll be bald in no time, but I feel sick whenever I think of the gold."

"That's no surprise. Living through that robbery and the accident must have been one hell of a scary experience for a five-year-old." He took her hands and tugged them away from her mouth. "It'll probably come to you when you relax," he said. "You were under so much pressure over the past month, with everyone pushing you about the gold, you might have developed a subconscious block against it."

"Maybe."

"You said you wanted to fill in the missing pieces about your father anyway. Seems to me, you can use those clippings you saved as a starting point."

She nodded. "That sounds more reasonable than cutting my hair."

"If you like, once you figure out the destination, I can get you there." He lifted her hands and brushed a light kiss across her knuckles. "We professional tour guides are good at that."

He was a toucher, she reminded herself. She shouldn't read more into this caress than there was. "Thank you, Derek. You're being more than generous."

"Nah. I just can't resist a challenge," he drawled. "Who knows? Finding a fortune in lost gold might be as much of a rush as shooting the Colca."

She smiled, feeling a pleasant thump in her pulse. "It might."

"But before we go any further, for the record, your father lied about your looks."

"What?"

"You are beautiful."

She tugged her hands free and rolled her eyes. "Derek…"

"Hasn't any man told you how pretty you are?"

"Well, no. Why should they?"

"What about your boyfriends?"

"Between running the store and taking care of my father, I didn't have much time for boyfriends."

Derek hesitated, his gaze searching hers. "You've never had a boyfriend?"

Admitting to him that she had never flown had made her enough of an oddity already. She tried to backpedal. "Actually, I did go out with the man who ran the florist shop next to the bookstore. We saw each other for years."

"You dated a florist?"

"Yes. Benjamin and I got along very well."

"Did Benjamin tell you how good you look in the mornings?"

"It didn't come up."

"Well, it's coming up now. Until I met you, I never thought that beige fleece could be sexy, and I'm not saying that to be nice."

"This really isn't—"

"Because if I was nice, I would be reminding myself that I'm your friend instead of thinking about all the things I would like to do with you."

The old Lydia would run. She would slam the door, make excuses for her racing pulse and hide from the feelings that were uncoiling inside her.

But Lydia didn't yet want to run from Derek. The way he was studying her, with his brows lowered and the beautiful lake-blue of his eyes darkened, was setting off bursts of pleasure along her nerves. Regardless of what the reality was, he made her *feel* pretty. Desirable. It was a heady sensation, as invigorating as cutting her hair.

"What…" She hardly recognized the low, throaty voice as her own. There wasn't the slightest trace of a squeak. "What kinds of things, Derek?"

"For starters, I'd like to see what goes with that red strap I can see at your shoulder."

She lifted her hand to her neckline and encountered the lacy edge of a bra strap. "I didn't know it showed."

"That's why it's so interesting. You're not doing it deliberately." He touched his fingers to the back of her hand. "I get the feeling you have no idea how attractive you are."

"Derek…"

"You're like this red lace," he said, tracing the edge of her sweatshirt neckline with his thumb. "You try to hide it under yards of beige fleece, but it shows anyway as soon as someone takes the time to look."

Her skin tingled from the touch of his thumb, while the thought of him looking made her breasts swell against her lace cups. "I can't believe we're talking about my underwear."

"Why not? I've been wondering about it since I saw it fall out of your gym bag."

"Uh…"

"It's a fascinating choice for a woman who likes to dress in beige." He smiled. "I think there's a hell of a lot more to you than meets the eye, Lydia."

She focused on his mouth. "Funny, that's what I was thinking about you, Derek."

"You were?"

"You're much more than just the good-looking cowboy I thought you were at first. You're a very sensitive man. I'm glad that…" She paused and tilted her head. A series of chimes, like a melody from a distant bell tower, drifted through the corridor. "What's that?"

Derek's smile faded. "Aw, hell," he muttered, straightening up.

Lydia looked around. The lights were flickering in rhythm with the chimes, which were increasing in volume. "What's going on?"

"It's the alarm," he said. "Someone's coming up the drive." He spun on his heel and headed down the corridor at a jog, twisting backward briefly to point at her. "Stay in your room until I see who it is."

She listened as Derek's footsteps faded around the bend of the corridor, then she stepped back into her room, closed the door and pressed her back to the wood panels. Her gaze fell on the painting that hung over the bed, one of the elegant, sensuous nudes. From this angle, the woman's smile appeared to be mocking.

Gritting her teeth, Lydia hitched her sweatshirt into place on her shoulder. The interruption was a timely reminder, exactly what she needed to get her thoughts back to her priorities, except that once again she felt like throwing something.

The security program was working as it was designed. The view on the monitor was automatically switching from one surveillance camera to the next as the intruder's progress was tracked. Derek dropped into the chair at the control console and swiveled to face the keyboard. He punched in the sequence that would jump ahead to the view from the gates.

A low-slung black sedan moved into the center of the screen and stopped when it reached the brick post that held the gate controls. Sunshine reflecting from the front windshield obscured the interior, but as Derek watched, the window of the driver's door lowered. He quickly adjusted the camera for maximum zoom and focused it on the open window.

The vehicle appeared to have only one occupant. A dark-haired man, his eyes hidden by a pair of designer sunglasses, turned directly toward the camera. He lifted one leather-gloved hand from the wheel in a lazy wave.

Derek swore under his breath and shut off the chimes. He hit the switch for the speaker that was built into the post. "You always did know how to make an entrance, Johnny."

The driver tipped down his sunglasses, revealing eyes that were as dark as his hair. "With the countermeasures that are installed at this place, I thought it would be wise not to sneak up on you. Do me a favor and deactivate the perimeter system, would you?"

Derek entered the disarming code as he had requested. John Kipling was familiar with the security at every one of Tony's houses—after all, he'd designed the systems. "Okay, it's off," Derek said.

John extended his arm to the keypad and the gates slid open. "I'll fill you in on what I've heard when I get to the house."

"I have a guest, John."

He arched one eyebrow. "Can I assume your hunting trip was a success?"

Derek glanced over his shoulder before replying. He'd left the door to the office open and couldn't be sure whether or not Lydia had obeyed his order to stay in her bedroom—her sneakers wouldn't make much noise on the stone floor. And if she had obeyed him, she likely wouldn't for long. He was rapidly learning that she wasn't as timid as she thought she was.

He returned his gaze to the monitor. "Go to the back door. I'll meet you there."

"Understood." The window rolled upward as the car moved ahead.

A few minutes later, Derek emerged from the staircase that had been cut through the rock behind the garage. John stood in the shadow of a fir tree near the edge of the cliff, his hands tucked into his pants pockets and his tie flapping across his chest in the breeze. Although it was only a few minutes after nine on a Saturday morning, he wore a charcoal gray wool suit and mirrorshined shoes. He appeared to be completely absorbed in the view, but Derek knew that John was aware of everything around him.

As if to verify his thought, John pivoted away from the tree and walked forward before Derek could say a word. As usual, he didn't waste time with small talk. He shook hands with Derek, then got straight down to business. "The Brotherhood's been unusually quiet," he said. "I haven't been able to pick up any electronic communications, so they must be doing face-to-face meetings. I'd say that indicates they're planning something big."

Derek nodded toward the drive and started walking. "Have you heard whether they're trying to establish another drug connection?"

"I've seen no evidence of it." John fell into step beside him. He was the same height as Derek and easily matched his stride. Although he looked as if he could have stepped from the cover of *GQ,* the way he moved resembled a panther's prowl rather than a model's strut. "That's not surprising. After what happened with their last supplier," he said, "the Colonel likely doesn't want to go that route again."

John was referring to the deal the Brotherhood had had with Stephan Volski. They had made obscene profits distributing Volski's heroin across the West, but the deal had dried up with the collapse of Volski's empire. Furthermore, their connection to Volski had brought the authorities to the Brotherhood's doorstep, causing them to abandon their South Dakota stronghold.

"Any leads on where they're building their new headquarters?" Derek asked.

"Regrettably, no. I've dealt with some tight organizations in my day, but these men are fanatics about security."

"None of my contacts at the bureau have anything, either, mainly because the Brotherhood isn't their top priority. Tony was right. The FBI are underestimating the seriousness of the threat the group poses."

"Amateurs," John muttered. "The feds should have realized that a direct raid on the stronghold would send the Colonel underground. They have no idea whom they're dealing with."

"And you do?"

John slanted him a look over the top of his sunglasses, then reached into his jacket and withdrew a compact disc. He handed it to Derek. "The Colonel's name is Hart McAllister, born sixty years ago in Childress, Texas. I put what facts I found on here."

Derek took the disc. He knew better than to ask John how he'd come by the information. John Kipling's sources were as nameless as the firm he used to work for. "Thanks."

"It's what I do, Derek. I expect you to pay back the favor someday."

"Geez, Johnny. You've got as much heart as Tony."

"I'll take that as a compliment." John tucked his tie back into his jacket and started toward his parked sedan. "Your hunch about the Colonel's background was right," he said. "The man who heads the Brotherhood used to be a real Colonel. He did three tours of duty in Vietnam in the late sixties."

"Was he wounded?"

"You pegged that right, too. He was caught in an artillery barrage of friendly fire and shipped home."

"How bad was his injury?"

"His left leg was shattered. He spent ten months in a VA hospital in Amarillo, did a year of therapy, but never got the full use of the leg back."

"That's plenty of time to nurse a grudge against the government and the military."

"He's got more than enough cause for a grudge. He went back to the family ranch when he finished his treatment, but he couldn't work it because of his bum leg. The county took it over for back taxes. After that he had a string of arrests for fraud and petty theft. Nine years ago he skipped parole after serving time for a firearms violation. There's no record of him since."

Derek whistled through his teeth. "Sounds like a recipe for one dangerous man."

"You were right about his profile, but I haven't been able to find any connection to the bullion. McAllister might be pursuing that strictly for the money after all. With the collapse of the Brotherhood's heroin connection, they're hungry for funds."

"There has to be more to it. I'm certain McAllister's determination to track down the bullion is personal. Otherwise he wouldn't have invested this much time in something that's a long shot. It's out of character."

John stopped when he reached his car and leaned a hip on the front fender. "You better hope you're right. You've invested a lot of time in this gold angle yourself."

"I know in my gut it's the key to bringing the Colonel out in the open."

"Only as long as you get to it first. If that gold falls into the hands of the Brotherhood, it's going to buy a load of misery."

"I won't let that happen."

"Are you making progress with Zachary's daughter?"

Without warning, Derek saw Lydia as she'd been before John had set off the alarm. Her cheeks had been flushed and her eyes darkened with awakening desire. He could still feel the gentle rasp of that lace strap against his thumb.

He picked up a rock from the drive and turned it over in his fingers, needing something to occupy his hands. Before he'd gotten sidetracked, she'd been talking about the gold, just as he had hoped. That was what he'd been nudging her toward for the past day. He should have pursued that with her immediately instead of returning to the topic of how pretty she was.

Damn that Zack Dorland. Had he realized how much damage his need to stay hidden had done to his daughter's self-image? Hadn't he cared how his lies had affected her? Repressing that woman's sexuality might have been his worst crime.

Derek pitched the rock at a tree. He was in no position to criticize anyone for lying. "It's going exactly as I had planned," he replied.

"How much have you told her?"

"Not much. Initially, I was concerned she wouldn't react well to the truth. Now I have to play out the hand."

"Giving information on a need-to-know basis always works for me," John commented. "It shouldn't be hard for someone with your skills to handle a woman like

Zack's daughter. From what the papers have said about the mouse, she's not the most sophisticated—"

"Don't call her that."

John took off his sunglasses and met Derek's gaze. His dark eyes glittered warningly. "I meant no offense."

"Yeah, but the press does."

"Fine. Take it up with them. In the meantime, I would strongly suggest that you let go of my suit."

Derek looked down and saw that he had a fistful of charcoal-gray wool in his hand. He spread his fingers and stepped back, alarmed by his lapse. He thrived on taking chances, but messing with John Kipling... "Sorry, John."

John regarded him silently for a minute, then replaced his sunglasses, smoothed the front of his jacket and opened the car door. "I charge for information, but I'll give you this advice for free," he said, picking up a pair of driving gloves from the seat. He pulled them on and got behind the wheel. "Pay less attention to the woman and more to your priorities, Derek. Tony isn't as forgiving as I am."

It was the reminder he needed. Derek watched the sedan drive through the gates, then turned and regarded the house. Technically, the house belonged to Tony, but after seven years, Derek considered it his home. It was the same with the business he'd sweated to build—on paper, it belonged to Tony, and like any banker, Tony could take it all away if Derek failed to repay what he owed.

Except, Tony wasn't a banker. Money didn't interest him, since he had more than he could spend in ten lifetimes.

Derek had glossed over the details when he'd told Lydia about Tony Monaco yesterday. Tony didn't want money from Derek—in return for helping Derek remain on the right side of the law, Tony expected him to bring another criminal to justice.

It was an unconventional way to repay a loan, but there was nothing conventional about Tony Monaco. The agreement he'd made with Derek wasn't unique. He'd done the same with John Kipling and countless others. It was the basis of Payback, the network Tony had established ten years ago as his personal justice campaign. Each member of Payback promised to repay the second chance Tony had given them by stopping someone else who had eluded the law.

In Derek's case, Tony had chosen the Canyon Brotherhood as the target of his justice. Once the organization was smashed and the Colonel and his accomplices behind bars, Derek's debt to Tony would be paid in full.

But if Derek didn't succeed in repaying Tony, he would lose everything that Tony had given him. He'd be right back where he'd been seven years ago, with no money and no protection. He'd be once more on the run from a loan shark who was out for blood...

Yeah, it was the reminder he needed. Clenching his jaw, Derek returned to the house.

Chapter 5

The mountain range spread out to the horizon in rippling waves of rock, a raw testament to the power of the forces that had formed them. Patches of forest growth clung to the slopes of the valley below, the majestic trees thrusting skyward in an exuberant burst of life. Lydia couldn't seem to get the smile off her face. "I love it!" she shouted.

Derek tapped her knee to get her attention, then pointed to the microphone that was attached to his helmet. "Swing yours down like this," he said. His voice came through her helmet earphones, sounding tinny against the racket of the engine. "I'll be able to hear you better."

She touched the side of her head, then adjusted the thin arm that held her microphone so that it sat in front of her chin. "This is fantastic," she said.

"You're not feeling queasy?"

"Not in the least. It's like a dream come true."

"Do you have dreams about flying?"

"Not often, but when I do, I absolutely love them. I do my best not to wake up." She raised her arms. "I spread my arms and soar, just as we're doing now. When I breathe in, I'd go up. When I exhale, I'd go down."

"Okay, inhale."

She glanced at him. A pair of reflective, aviator-style glasses hid his eyes, but she could see the hint of a smile dimple his cheeks. Lifting her head, she drew in a deep breath.

He moved the lever that he grasped with his left hand, and at the same time pulled back on the stick he held with his right. The pitch of the motor changed, the nose tipped up and the helicopter began a smooth climb.

Lydia laughed, delighted, as she watched the ground recede. "Wonderful."

"It gets better. Blow it out slowly."

She pursed her lips and exhaled.

Derek adjusted the controls again and the helicopter swooped downward toward the side of the valley. The trees that had looked so far away seconds ago loomed toward them with heart-stopping speed. Seconds before a collision seemed inevitable, Derek moved the stick to the left and the helicopter veered safely past.

Lydia pressed her hands to her stomach. "Derek!"

He leveled the craft out and turned to follow the path of the river that wound along the valley floor. "Are you having fun yet?"

She moved her hands to her chest. Her heart was pounding hard enough to feel through her jacket. She could barely catch her breath. "You scared me half to death."

"Really?" He grinned. "You're still smiling."

He was right, she realized. The thrill of that dive hadn't been unpleasant at all. "Is that what you do with your clients?"

"Only if they ask me to. And not when the bird is fully loaded."

She twisted in her seat to study the helicopter. She couldn't remember the name of the model he'd said it was, but it appeared to be capable of carrying several passengers. There were seats beside the windows along the sides of the narrow fuselage and an area at the back that would serve for storing gear. Unlike the Jeep he'd driven the other day, this helicopter was painted with the name of Derek's company.

Although he'd acted casual when he'd assisted her into the helicopter, she'd seen the pride in his expression when she'd commented on the sign. It was obvious to her that he truly loved the business he'd founded—this meant more to him than simply a way to make a living.

And why shouldn't it? she thought, returning her gaze to the scene that unrolled beyond the windshield. This tour business represented Derek's ability to start a new life. She admired the way he'd channeled the desire for risk that had led to his gambling problem into something constructive.

"You've gone quiet all of a sudden," Derek said. "Are you still feeling okay?"

"I'm fine, thanks. Really, I shouldn't have said that you scared me. You didn't."

"Okay. Hang on, I'm going to set this thing down."

She leaned closer to the window, but she could see nothing except trees and steep rock slopes. Sunshine glittered from the shallow river that sped beneath them. She was about to ask him where they would land when the river split in two to flow around a large slab of flat rock. Derek slowed to a hover when they reached the center of the island, and Lydia realized it was much larger than it had first appeared. There was ample room to land more than one helicopter.

Ten minutes later, Lydia was thankful for the warmth of her jogging suit, dowdy or not. The breeze that swept across the water from the valley was brisk. She put her hands in her jacket pockets and turned away from the helicopter to survey the island. Like the clearing where she'd awakened a few days ago, the scene that spread out before her was as beautiful as a postcard.

Yet a photograph couldn't have duplicated the scene's impact on the rest of her senses. It was like the difference between the books she read and real life.

Along with the brisk breeze came the scents of water, sun-warmed rock and pine. Added to that were the sounds: the gurgle of the river in front of her, the soft ticking of cooling metal from the aircraft behind her and the familiar tread of Derek's boots as he walked over to join her.

"Sometimes I come fishing here when I'm not busy," Derek said. He pointed to a ledge of rock that was darkened with moisture. "There's usually a trout sitting under the ripples right off that spot."

"That sounds like a tame sport for someone with your tastes."

"You haven't seen the size of the trout. Do you like to fish?"

"I've never tried it." She shook her head. "That sounds so pathetic. I didn't get out much, did I?"

"That's understandable."

"Is it? I don't know. I had thought I was happy the

way things were, but now that I've left my old life behind, I'm realizing how restrictive it was."

Derek put his sunglasses in his jacket pocket and turned up the collar. "Your father made a prison for himself and brought you up to share it. It's only because you're free that you're able to look back and see the bars."

She tilted her head to study him, struck by the simple truth of what he'd just said. He'd described her life in a nutshell. "You're a very insightful man, Derek."

"Insightful," he mumbled. "You've already called me decent and sensitive. Now I'm going to have to do something manly like pound my chest or burp."

She laughed. "How do you do that?"

"What?"

"You hardly know me, but you always seem to know the right thing to say. Are you sure you're not an expert in psychology?"

"It's a gift." He put his hand on the small of her back and guided her forward. "Since you didn't fish, and you didn't go for helicopter rides, what did you do for fun?"

"I read," she said, moving beside him as they walked toward the ledge he'd pointed out. "I also belonged to a health club and swam a few times a week. I love the water. And for a while, I used to do volunteer work at the hospital, too. My dad told me my mother used to be a nurse."

"Did you ever want to do that?"

"Oh, I couldn't have, I have a strong aversion to blood. I helped out by reading stories in the children's ward, but I had to give that up when I took over the store."

"You gave up a lot for your father," he commented. "Did the two of you travel anywhere?"

"Not often. He claimed he got carsick. And as I said before, we never flew."

"How did he like to spend his time?"

"After he got ill and couldn't get out much, he liked to watch movies. He was a real fan of Westerns."

"Any in particular?"

"We had the complete John Wayne collection and all the old Audie Murphy movies. Oh, and he watched those old Clint Eastwood ones so much, he wore out the tapes. I was gradually replacing his tape collection with DVDs, but some of the older films were hard to find." She paused as they neared the river's edge. "I wonder if there's a connection between his fondness for Westerns and the bullion robbery."

"Did he ever comment on the films?"

"Not that I can recall." She squeezed her eyes closed and tried to remember what her father had said about the movies, but she couldn't come up with anything.

"What are you doing?" Derek asked.

She opened her eyes and sighed. "Trying to jog my memory."

Derek slipped his arm around her shoulder. "I'm no shrink, but seems to me you'd get further if you don't try to force it. Let's talk about something else."

She waited for him to drop his arm. When he didn't, she fitted herself closer to his side, grateful for the extra warmth.

Oh, who was she fooling? She was enjoying being close to him, regardless of the reason. The more time they spent together, the more she realized she was rapidly developing a crush on this tall, handsome adventurer. Much of it was probably due to gratitude, since he had rescued her and was continuing to help her. He was also an uncommonly empathetic man. Being isolated with him in spectacularly romantic surroundings didn't hurt, either.

But she didn't have to look for excuses. She was certain that any woman, even someone with more experience than her, would be hard-pressed to remain unaffected by a man like this one. "Tell me about yourself, Derek," she said. "Where are you from? You mentioned that you lived in Las Vegas as a child, didn't you?"

"That's right, but I was born in Oklahoma City. That's where my parents were from."

"Ah. That explains the drawl. It's sexy, by the way."

He tipped an imaginary hat. "Why, thank you, ma'am," he said, exaggerating his twang.

She laughed. "When did you move to Nevada?"

"We moved there when I was around seven. I grew up in the Vegas casinos."

"*In* the casinos?"

"Yeah. My father worked as a blackjack dealer and my mother was a showgirl." He smiled crookedly. "Sounds like the beginning of a country song, doesn't it?"

"It must have been exciting."

"It was. They worked the major hotels on the strip. Babysitters were expensive, so my mother used to leave me backstage while she worked. It didn't take me long to find ways to sneak into the casinos so I could watch the action."

"I've only seen them on TV, but I imagine all that glitz must have been fascinating to a child. That might have been why…" She hesitated, wondering whether she had the right to make such a personal comment.

"Why I became a gambling addict? Don't worry, the thought occurred to me, too. I grew up around gambling, so that's probably why I turned to it as a way to fill my needs."

"Do your parents still live in Las Vegas?"

"No. My dad was killed by a drunk driver when I was ten. A year after that, my mother walked away one night after a show and never came back."

She turned and placed her hands on his chest. "Oh, Derek, I'm sorry. That must have been horrible for you. What did you do?"

"I hid out in the casino for almost two weeks, waiting for her to come back." He chuckled. "I had some guts for a kid. I slept in the lounges and pretended my parents were hotel guests so that I could eat, but the security staff caught on eventually."

"How can you laugh about that? It's terrible."

"Kids are survivors, but I guess I don't need to tell you that." He rested his hands on her shoulders. "Anyway, it was a long time ago. I got over it."

She tried to picture Derek as an eleven-year-old, but couldn't. In his scuffed boots and faded denim, with his sun-streaked hair tousled by the breeze, he was too decidedly a large, adult male. "Did your mother ever come back?" she asked.

He shook his head. "I went into the foster care system. I found out years later that she had eloped with a copier salesman who didn't want kids, which is why she left me. The last I heard, they were managing a trailer park in Florida."

Lydia had to bite her lip to keep from criticizing his mother. How could anyone abandon their child? Her father hadn't acted prudently when he'd taken her along on the robbery, but at least he hadn't considered leaving her behind.

If Lydia had a child, she would never leave her, she would protect her with her dying breath.

She trembled at a wave of cold. It wasn't from the

breeze, it was from something within, as if her mind had brushed against the wispy edge of a nightmare.

I love you, baby. Remember that. I don't want to leave you.

Derek took her hands and rubbed them between his palms. "What's wrong?"

The warmth of his touch pulled her back. She looked into his eyes, then impulsively stretched up to kiss his cheek.

"What was that for?"

She wasn't sure. It wouldn't make much sense to tell him that she'd felt a sudden need for human contact. "I guess I did it because I could. I don't normally do things like that, but I didn't think you'd mind, since you always seem to be touching me. But if you'd prefer that I don't—"

As he had once before, he ended the conversation by settling his mouth over hers.

She closed her eyes and swayed into him, feeling light-headed with the pleasure that spread over her. She'd wondered whether his kiss would taste as good the second time. As impossible as it seemed, it was better.

And his kiss really was nothing like Benjamin's. Derek's lips were supple, not stiff. He seemed completely at ease, as if he had all the time in the world, with nothing else to do except enjoy this moment. When his nose nudged into her glasses, he paused only long enough to lift them off, then resumed the kiss as easily as he'd started it. He moved his mouth along hers, drawing on her lower lip, then dipping his tongue between them as he tried out different angles and pressures. Lydia absorbed it all, then shyly rubbed her tongue alongside his.

At her response, Derek groaned. She not only heard the sound, she felt it vibrate against her breasts. When had she moved closer? Through the layers of clothes between them, she could feel the solid warmth of his chest. Her heart was pounding as it had when they'd been in the helicopter and had been swooping toward those trees, yet it was anticipation she felt, not fear.

She felt safe with Derek. It was strange, since everything about him was completely foreign to the safety she used to crave. She slid her hands into his hair, reveling in its silky glide between her fingers. She traced his ears the same way he'd traced hers that morning, delighted to discover that he shuddered when she touched the lobes. Lifting on her toes, she broke off the kiss and pulled his head down so that she could close her lips around his earlobe.

He whispered an oath. It was one she'd never heard him use before, a short, crude word that blended with the sound of the river and the breeze, increasing the excitement she felt. No, it was more than excitement, it was power. Acting instinctively, she rubbed her teeth across his ear, then pressed an open-mouthed kiss to the side of his neck.

"Lydia." He drew his head back. "Slow down."

She blinked. His face was inches away, his gaze searing into hers. Tension hardened the lean angles of his jaw, yet his lips were still moist and parted, as if he were on the verge of kissing her again. "I'm sorry," she murmured. "I thought you would like that."

"Like it?" He placed one hand on her buttocks and drew her against his lower body. "Liking it isn't the problem. It's what we do about it."

A reckless thrill went through her as she felt the stiff bulge of his erection against her stomach. Clearly, she wasn't the only one affected by their kiss. "I, uh, didn't mean to make you uncomfortable."

"You did nothing wrong."

"Well, you did want to stop." She hesitated, struck by a sudden thought. "I should have realized it," she said, twisting free from his grasp. "You have a girl-friend, don't you?"

"What?"

"I misread your signals. All that flirting you do, you were just being friendly, weren't you?" She pressed her palms to her cheeks as she continued to back away. Pebbles slid under the soles of her sneakers, grating across the rock. "This is embarrassing."

He muttered another oath and closed the distance be-tween them in two strides. "Lydia, you didn't misread anything. I don't have a girlfriend. I'm not seeing any-one." He angled his head to look into her eyes. "But I told you I didn't expect this. I hope you realize this isn't why I brought you home with me."

"I know. You made it clear. I shouldn't have—"

"No, I started it. I know I should keep my hands off you, but I never seem to be able to."

She glanced at his hands and saw that he was still holding her glasses. She snatched them from him, fit-ted them on her nose and looked toward the helicopter. "Can we go back now? This discussion is getting very awkward."

"We're not going anywhere until we get this straight. I realize this isn't a pleasure trip for you. You've gone through a major upheaval in your life and I don't want to add to it. Whether you believe it or not, I'm trying to protect you."

"Great. Just like my father. He wanted to protect me so he kept me wrapped up in a cocoon. Just like Benjamin. He probably thought I would scurry for the nearest mousehole if he dared to take off my glasses when he kissed me." She swung her arm to gesture to the valley around them. "I never knew how much I would like it out here. I didn't know I liked to fly. There are so many things I haven't done, sometimes it makes me so frustrated I want to scream, but of course, I never do, because I never have."

Although she hadn't shouted, her words seemed to linger in the air, blending with the sounds of the wilderness. Lydia crossed her arms tightly and lifted her face to let the breeze cool her cheeks.

She felt Derek approach more than she heard him. He stood behind her, not touching, and yet every cell in her body was strumming with the awareness of how close he was. She kept her gaze on the shimmering water. "All this freedom to do what I want seems to be going to my head. You're an outrageously attractive man, Derek, so I thought you wouldn't mind..." She stopped. "Could we put this behind us and move on?"

Derek struggled not to reach for her. His stomach knotted with a potent mix of anger at her father and compassion for her. He'd known how she'd lived, and he'd felt the innocence in her kisses, but he hadn't wanted to carry the thought through to its logical conclusion.

Now he did. Even someone who wasn't a trained profiler could see that Lydia was a virgin. The fact wasn't surprising, yet his reaction was. He'd believed he was a rational man, in control of his emotions, so the wave of desire he felt took him off guard. It was dark and primitive, an urge to possess her as much as to protect her. He wanted to show her where her kisses could lead, and he'd make sure that she liked it.

He knew he shouldn't let the situation get more complicated than it already was. He couldn't lose sight of his objectives. The Colonel, the Brotherhood and his debt to Tony were his priorities.

But if he did the right thing and kept his distance, she would think it was a personal rejection. She was just starting to break out of her shell. The last thing he wanted was to add to the damage her father had already done.

Damn, who was he fooling? There was no point trying to excuse his lack of self-control by dressing it up as something noble. He hadn't been able to keep away from her yet.

He moved closer, fitting her back to his chest so he could rest his chin on the top of her head. As soon as he touched her, a wave of relief spread through his body. This felt right. His head might be muttering objections, but his instincts were shouting approval. In spite of his agenda, this was one aspect of his relationship with Lydia that he could be honest about.

"I enjoyed the way you nibbled my ear," he said. "I'd be lying if I said I didn't want you to do it again."

She didn't respond, but some of the stiffness eased from her shoulders.

"And for the record," he continued, "I didn't ask you to stop, I only asked you to slow down. I don't want you to look back on this later and think I took advantage of the circumstances."

"I appreciate your concern, Derek, but I'm a grown woman and I'd truly hate it if you say something about protecting me again."

"I won't." He tilted his head to blow lightly across her curls. "I could have the best intentions in the world, but that won't make what's happening between us go away."

"It's all right. I'm not naive enough to think that a few kisses mean anything."

"They were dynamite kisses, Lydia. I've been trying to be your friend since we met, because that's what you need, but it's not working."

"We're very different people."

He took her by the shoulders and turned her to face him. "Sure, we're different. That's why we've got sparks."

"Sparks?"

He rubbed his thumb along her lower lip, picking up the moisture from their kiss. He smiled as he saw her pupils expand. "Oh, yeah. We've got major sparks, and now that you've told me it's mutual, I can't see much point in fighting it."

"Derek…"

"I'm still not expecting anything from you, Lydia. I know you're trying to get your life back together, and you're only staying with me until we find your father's gold." He moved his thumb from her mouth to his and tasted the moisture he'd picked up. "But that doesn't mean we can't enjoy ourselves while you're here, does it?"

She caught her breath at his gesture, then touched the tip of her tongue to her lip.

"The next time you kiss me," he said, "I'm not going to be the one to put on the brakes."

He waited, watching her face as she digested what he had said. For a while, it seemed to Derek that she was considering whether or not to run. Finally, though, her mouth twitched into the beginning of a smile. Her eyes sparkled with a hint of the same interest he'd been catching glimpses of for days. "What makes you think I'm going to kiss you again at all?" she asked.

"You did say I'm outrageously attractive, didn't you?"

"I'm sure you don't need me to tell you that. Plenty of women must have already."

"Not that many. And never one who wears red lace under her sweats."

Her cheeks pinkened.

His smile grew. Yeah, his instincts were right. "The florist was an idiot."

"What?"

"Benjamin. He should never have let you go."

He'd meant to make her feel better. Instead, his remark dimmed her sparkle. "He was clever enough, Derek," she said. "He dated me for several years and had managed to find one reason after another to keep, well, putting on the brakes. I suppose I let him string me along because I saw him as my best chance to escape my father's prison."

Derek moved his knuckles to her cheek, feeling a familiar mix of anger and compassion. More than anything, he wanted to banish that self-doubt from her face. "You're freeing yourself on your own, Lydia."

"Maybe I am. Everything changed after my father died. Benji was suddenly very attentive. He even offered me a ring."

"He proposed?"

"You sound as surprised as I was, but he hadn't lost his mind when he proposed to me. As I said, he was quite clever."

"I didn't mean it like that."

"He'd believed that if he was my husband, he'd get half of everything I had." She lifted her chin and fitted her glasses more snugly to her nose, as she often did when she was trying to gather her courage. "I turned him down. It wouldn't take a genius to figure it out. He didn't want me, he wanted the go—" Her words cut off on a gasp. Her hand shook, knocking her glasses askew.

Derek scanned the area quickly, but there was nothing out of place. He grasped her elbow to steady her. "What is it?" he asked. "What's wrong?"

She blinked, her gaze coming back into focus. "I saw her again. That red-haired woman."

"Your mother?"

"I hope not," she whispered.

"Why?"

Her lips trembled. "Derek, I think she was dead."

Hart squinted into the glare as the sun set beyond the mountain peak, trying to minimize the pain that knifed through his head from the slanting rays. Lately, the headaches were coming more frequently, but he wanted to witness the loading. This was a historic day, the beginning of the Brotherhood's own place in history.

The ambulance gleamed golden as it was backed toward the ore mill that now served as the Brotherhood's armory. Men moved into action immediately, transferring the explosives to the vehicle with commendable zeal. They understood what was at stake, too. The years of preparation, of patient waiting, were almost over. There was no turning back. A man who'd had everything he valued taken away, who had nothing left to lose, was the most deadly fighter on the planet.

"Colonel?"

Hart twisted away from the window and returned the salute of the soldier who stood in the doorway. "Yes, Private?"

"I'm here to pick up the statement."

He gestured to the envelope on his desk. The manifesto he'd penned was as vital a part of this operation as the cargo that was being loaded outside. It was their declaration of war.

The noise of the man's boots seemed like cannon fire, setting off another wave of agony behind Hart's eyes. He waited until the man had left, then closed the door and shuffled to his cot. The creaking springs sounded like screams. His nostrils flared as he inhaled slowly to battle the pain.

He knew how to manage physical weakness. He'd lived with the reminder of how to do that in his leg for more than half his life now. This headache would pass, as they always did. But it was important not to let the men see him like this. He couldn't let the troops lose confidence in their leader, not when they were this close to the final campaign.

Hart gritted his teeth against a renewed burst of pain. It was difficult to focus under conditions like these, so he let his mind drift. As it often happened these days, it turned to the past. To the gold—and the woman—that should have been his.

He remembered her face as she had leaned over his bed. She'd been his angel, taking away his pain with her gentle hands. His heart had beaten faster merely at the sound of her footsteps. Her laughter had seemed to glitter, drawing him from the darkness.

His beautiful Rose, with her irrepressible hair and her mischievous smile. He'd loved her with every fibre of his being. She had given him a reason to wake up each day, to endure the indignity of being warehoused in that hospital with the rest of the army castoffs, no longer fit for duty, yet not fit for anything else. It was because of Rose that he'd gone through the torture of rehab. He'd willed himself to walk again for her.

Yet like the country he'd loved, she had turned her back on him, too. Rose had thought she would run away.

But the last time he'd seen her, she had been the one who couldn't walk.

Chapter 6

The answering machine at the back of Derek's desk clicked on, sending his voice through the room. "You've reached On the Edge Tours. Leave a message. If I get back alive, I'll get back to you."

Lydia turned away from the window to see if Derek was going to pick up this call. He was sitting in front of a computer table that was within arm's reach of his desk, but he kept his attention on the monitor in front of him.

A man's voice came from the speaker. "Hey, there, li'l buddy. It's Eddie. Thought you'd be back by now. You doin' a Trango climb next year? Save me a spot."

The message was similar to the other four that had come in over the course of the morning. From the sound of it, Derek had no shortage of potential customers. This was the third man who had asked about something called Trango.

Of all the rooms Lydia had seen in the house so far, Derek's office bore the most traces of his presence. The shelf beneath the window held rolled maps, stacks of brochures and boxes of black T-shirts with his company name emblazoned in silver, as well as a slender, deadly-looking tool he'd said was a climbing axe. A huge cork bulletin board on one wall was peppered with Polaroid photos of everything from rock-strewn rapids to cliffs made of ice, each one bearing a label scrawled in black marker. Printouts of what appeared to be satellite photographs overflowed from his desk to the chair that sat in front of it and a coil of gray-and-blue striped rope rested in one corner on the stone floor like a pet snake.

More than the brochures or the helicopter, Derek's office brought home the reality of what he did for a living. Lydia had enjoyed flying yesterday—as she had told him, it was like her favorite dream—yet seeing the rest of the places he'd been was disconcerting. He really was very different from her in so many ways.

Sure, we're different. That's why we've got sparks.

Lydia moved her gaze along Derek's back, admiring the perfect taper from his shoulders to his narrow waist. Oh, he was a gorgeous man. Even unshaven, rumpled and bent over a computer keyboard, he was still appealing. He couldn't help it. His lean body, his tousled hair, the way he held himself like a relaxed predator, all of it was so sexy, he gave her goose bumps.

Things had changed since they'd returned from the river yesterday. Derek seemed to regard this attraction between them as something completely natural, no big deal. True to his word, he was taking things slow, leaving the choice of what happened up to her. He hadn't kissed her again, but he'd continued to touch her. A soft brush of his fingertip against her cheek, a light squeeze when his hand touched her shoulder. It astonished her how stimulating the most casual contact could be.

Yet if she was honest with herself, deep down inside she'd been hoping for something like this since the morning she'd awakened in his Jeep. It was likely the real reason she'd agreed to come home with him. Why shouldn't she enjoy herself while she was here?

A shocking thought for a mouse, wasn't it?

"Lydia, I can't find any record of your mother or her death," he said, swiveling his chair away from the computer. "I've tried under Hobbs, Smith and Dorland."

She glanced at the envelope of papers she'd brought to the office earlier. "I realize my birth certificate would have to be a fake, since my father's real name isn't Smith. I guess I should have realized he would have to lie about my mother's maiden name, too."

"I'm sorry."

"Don't be. What's one more lie added to all the rest?"

He flinched at that, and Lydia immediately regretted complaining. He'd already been busy at the computer when she'd found her way here this morning. She hadn't intended to ask him for help, yet he'd put aside his own work and volunteered to track down information for her.

"I wish there was some way I could do what you're doing," she said. "But my computer skills are pretty limited. I would have no idea how to access the kind of databases you're getting into."

"No problem. I've done this before. Besides, I've installed some gadgets on this one that make it easy to get into places most hook-ups can't."

She looked at the array of electronic hardware that was set up along the back wall. There were several monitors, more keyboards and a bewildering tangle of cables. "Is that what you used to do?"

"What?"

"When you were…" She hesitated. "Did you work with computers before you started your tour company?"

"That's a good guess."

"You seem to be very skilled at this."

"Yeah. It still comes in handy with what I do now." He cocked his head to study her, his eyebrows lowering in concentration.

"Is something wrong?" she asked.

"What color are you wearing today?"

"What?" She glanced down at her sweatshirt. "I suppose you could call this taupe. It's halfway between beige and green."

One corner of his mouth tilted upward. "That's not what I meant."

An unexpected laugh rose to her throat. Only yesterday, talking about her underwear had felt terribly daring. Yet Derek was as matter-of-fact about flirting with her as he was about helping her jog her memories. Once again, he seemed to know the perfect approach to use in order to put her at ease. She tucked in her chin so she could peer at her shoulder.

"No, it's not showing," he said. "That's why I had to ask. Is it the red one again?"

She resisted the impulse to cross her arms—she'd been clumsy enough with her response the day before, and she didn't want to seem like a prude—yet her breasts were tingling, yearning to be touched.

"Well?" he asked.

Her pulse gave a pleasant thump at the challenge in his gaze. She smiled. "Peach," she said. "Peach satin."

He groaned and turned back to the computer. "Serves me right."

Still smiling, she strolled toward the bulletin board.

Oh, she was becoming thoroughly infatuated with this man, but what was wrong with that? Her sexuality was one aspect of herself that she'd never had the chance to explore in her old life.

Who better to show her unfamiliar territory than a professional tour guide?

"What's Trango?" she asked. "I couldn't help hearing your clients mention it."

"Trango Tower. It's a mountain in Pakistan. There should be a picture of it there." His fingers worked over the keyboard. "Look in the lower left corner."

It took her a minute to find. When she did, at first she thought the photograph had been tacked up sideways, but the snow-covered peaks in the background were upright. She was looking at a vertical wall of sheer rock. "Good Lord," she murmured. "People pay you to take them there? I'd pay you to take me away."

"You've got more courage than you think you do, Lydia," he said.

"That might not be my real name."

"No, if I were still a betting man, I'd bet you're a Lydia. Your father didn't change his first name. It's your mother's last name that's the issue."

She straightened the edge of the Trango Tower photo so that it lined up neatly with one of a cave. "Checking into my mother could turn out to be a waste of time. There's no logical reason to believe the woman I remembered yesterday is my mother."

"What does your gut tell you?"

"My gut?"

"Don't take time to analyze it, just go with what you feel." He glanced at her over his shoulder. "Trust your instincts. That's what I usually do."

For what had to be the hundredth time since yesterday, Lydia closed her eyes and tried to recall the woman's features, but nothing came. She was disappointed, of course, but part of her was relieved—she wasn't sure that she wanted to see that troubling image again.

Yet she hadn't really seen it, she'd felt it. The loss, the aching sadness, the sense that something was horribly wrong. It was like the utter finality of seeing her father's body in the morgue.

"Yes," she replied. "My gut tells me she was someone I loved. And there's…well, it's strange, like the way I thought I remembered the feel of her hair." She tapped her fingertips to her mouth. "I can remember what it felt like to say 'mommy.'"

"That's good enough for me. She's your mother."

"But this might not bring me any closer to my dad's gold. There wasn't any record that he was married at the time of the robbery. The police told me it was just the two of us. It wouldn't have made any sense for him to hide my mother's existence and not hide mine."

"I'll keep digging for information about your mother. We'll figure out where that memory of her fits. There must be some reason it's the one that's coming up."

"It might be faster if I saw a hypnotist," she muttered, only half joking. "I've been trying my best to recall more and I've gotten nowhere."

"Did the cops suggest hypnosis when they were questioning you?"

"They did, but I refused. They had already pushed me so hard about my father and the robbery, I felt sick when I thought about it."

"The mind can be a tricky thing. From the sound of it, those cops made the block on your memory worse."

"This is frustrating. Now that I want to remember, I can't."

"Hey, you spent twenty-four years trying not to. Nothing's going to change overnight. Those memories are probably hidden as well as the bullion."

"Why do you think my father never went back for it?" she asked.

"The gold?"

"Yes. If he went to the trouble of stealing it and hiding it, why would he live as frugally as we did instead of using it to buy us a better life?"

He swiveled his chair away from the computer once more to face her. "You're the one who knew him the best. Why do you think he left it?"

She moved to the desk and removed the papers from the chair so that she could sit, taking time to consider the question. "He hadn't seemed concerned with luxuries. Some of that could have been because he was worried about being noticed, but I don't remember him sounding dissatisfied with the life we had."

"Did he ever talk about his ambitions?"

"Only the bookstore. He'd told me that my mother had loved to read and had dreamed of opening a bookstore when she retired from nursing."

Derek leaned forward, resting his forearms on his thighs as he clasped his hands loosely between his knees. It was a relaxed pose, yet his gaze was sharp. "What else did he say about her?"

"She had a laugh that sounded like bells. He didn't talk about her very often, but when he did, I could hear the love in his voice. He called her his angel. I don't think he ever stopped mourning her."

"And yet he didn't keep her picture."

"No. Maybe it was too painful. He preferred landscapes. Nothing like the kind of art that Tony has, just prints of the sort of photographs you'd see on calendars."

"What kind of landscapes, Lydia?"

"Western scenes mostly. Big open prairies, buttes, ghost towns, that kind of thing. It went along with his taste in movies."

Derek looked thoughtful for a while. "Your father might have left the gold where it was because he felt remorse over the crime."

"That's possible," she agreed. "The man I knew was a stickler when it came to obeying the law. He was always lecturing me on what was the right way to behave. He wouldn't even let me take nine items into the eight-items-or-less line at the grocery store."

"That's got to be from more than just a need to keep a low profile. It sounds as if what he did ate at his conscience."

"I can understand why it would. According to the police and all the newspaper reports, my dad had worked in the assay lab at the precious metals refinery where the bullion shipment originated. He'd been a loyal employee for years. That's how he obtained the inside information that enabled him to hijack the truck. The driver never suspected a thing until my dad knocked him out."

"He betrayed the trust they had in him."

Something in Derek's tone made her glance up. He was looking at his clasped hands, his gaze distant. Belatedly, Lydia realized this could be a sensitive topic for him. She reached out to squeeze his hand. "Derek, I'm sorry. I've been so focused on how this is affecting me, I forget how it could be affecting you."

"Me?"

"There are parallels between you and my father."

"Because we were both crooks who went straight?"

"I wasn't going to put it like that."

"It's true. We both were honest citizens until we committed a crime. The main difference is that he didn't get caught."

Although he spoke casually, and his posture hadn't changed, she could feel the tension in his hands. "You believed you had no choice, Derek," she said.

"There's always a choice." He turned his hand over and clasped hers. "Some just aren't as easy to make."

"Well, I admire you for making the right one when you met Tony."

"Yeah. I owe him big-time." He ran his thumb along her knuckles. "But speaking of parallels, there had to be some reason why your father would decide to throw away all those years of loyalty to that refinery. Do you know if he gambled or was in debt?"

Her first response was to deny it, but she forced herself to consider the question. "I don't believe he was. He wasn't a risk-taker."

"Something made him act out of character. He burned his bridges when he decided to steal that bullion. The cops had no trouble figuring out it was him, so he would have to have planned to assume another identity all along. He knew he couldn't go back."

"Do you ever want to go back, Derek?"

He brought her hand to his lips and kissed her palm, then shook his head. "My bridges got burned too, Lydia."

"How?"

"Tony pulled a few strings to make sure I didn't get charged, but he couldn't keep my boss from finding out. She fired me. She also made sure everyone where I worked knew I'd been willing to break the law to feed my gambling habit. My reputation was shot. I wouldn't be able to go back to my old job if I wanted to."

"That doesn't seem fair."

"Don't waste your sympathy on me, Lydia. I like what I do now."

She stroked his cheek with the hand that he'd kissed. "Derek, when did it start?"

"What?"

"Your gambling. Not the habit itself, but the reason for it. Why did you start needing those adrenaline highs you get from risk?"

He took a moment to think about it. "I'm not sure, Lydia. Probably when I was a teenager. I started with skateboards and dirt bikes and things escalated from there."

"Was that when you were in a foster home?"

"That's right."

"Didn't your foster parents try to stop you?"

"There were a lot of other kids to keep them busy. As long as I didn't break too many bones, they were cool about it."

"My dad would have had a fit."

"Sure. That's because he cared."

And that, she realized, was the real answer. Losing both parents the way he had must have left a huge void in Derek's heart where love should have been. With no one to care, he would have found other ways to fill it.

What else could she do? She leaned forward and pressed her mouth to his.

His beard stubble tickled. It was an intimate sensation, pleasantly stimulating, making her vividly conscious of how, well, male he was. Yet this kiss was different from the others they'd shared, more tender than passionate. Although Lydia felt the familiar tingles dance across her nerves as she moved her lips over his, the true enjoyment of this kiss was more than physical. She wasn't thinking of how handsome Derek was, she was more interested in the glimpse he'd given her of the man inside.

She pulled back and looked into his eyes. Shadows stirred in the blue depths, hints of more aspects she had yet to uncover.

"It's funny, isn't it?" she murmured. "Not ha-ha funny but kind of sad. We had such different childhoods, mine overprotective, yours the opposite, but maybe that's why we…"

"We what?"

Oh, why not say it? she thought. "We fit."

His mouth quirked. "That's how men and women are built."

She felt a flush warm her cheeks. "I didn't mean fitting that way. I think we must have some kind of special bond, as if we're two sides of the same coin. Maybe that's why fate had you traveling down the same road I was."

He sobered, his gaze immediately shuttering.

Lydia bit her tongue. It looked as if she shouldn't have said it after all.

The phone rang. Seconds later, Derek's recorded voice came from the answering machine. There was a beep. The male voice that came from the speaker was heavily accented. "Derek, this is Jean-Paul. Are you making any plans to do the Colca before the rainy season?"

Derek reached across his desk for the phone. "Sorry, Lydia," he said. "I should take this one."

Lydia rose to her feet, grateful for the interruption.

A bond? What had she meant? That she was falling in *love?*

She was getting carried away again. They'd only known each other a few days. Love at first sight didn't happen in real life.

While Derek dealt with the call, Lydia wandered back to the bulletin board of photos to see if he'd had the chance to put up one of the Colca River. His customer was going to be disappointed to learn he'd missed the trip by a few weeks.

As had happened before, she was struck by how well Derek's choice of a new career suited him. Each one of those tour photos represented a victory over his gambling addiction. Thanks to Tony's intervention, he'd been given the opportunity to build a new life rather than building himself a mental prison the way her father had.

She glanced at the computer behind Derek. He displayed a knack for tracking down information, and he did have an analytical mind, yet she couldn't picture him being content to sit in front of a keyboard all day.

Which was probably why he'd had to turn to gambling to satisfy his need for excitement.

She returned her attention to the photos, going through the rows from left to right. There was a snapshot labeled "Colca River, Peru," after all. It was similar to a print of the Grand Canyon that had been in her father's study, but this one was narrower and deeper. Her gaze was snagged by a heap of gray boulders at the shore.

Frowning at the boulders, she leaned closer for a better look.

Derek ended his phone call and got to his feet. "Did you spot something interesting?"

"This looks familiar," she said. "It's strange. I know I haven't been there, but the shape of these rocks reminds me of something." She shook her head. "I don't know. The color's wrong."

Derek moved to the newspaper clippings that she'd left with her papers and rifled through them. "What color do you see in your memory?"

"A yellow-brown. I guess I'm remembering another one of my dad's pictures."

"Or maybe one of these?"

She went to look at the clipping he'd selected. It was a black-and-white photo of the gully where the wrecked truck had been found. She must have looked at it a hundred times, yet somehow it was tugging at her… "That's what I must have been thinking of."

"You said the rocks were yellow-brown. Was it sunny?"

"Yes, it was a hot day."

"What did it smell like?"

She spoke without thinking. "Diesel fuel."

As soon as the words left her lips, Lydia turned away from the photo, her heart pounding. "I can't understand why I said that."

Derek stroked her hair. "You're remembering something, Lydia. There's nothing to be afraid of."

"I'm not afraid. I—"

"I'll keep you safe." He settled his hand between her shoulders and gently drew her toward him. "Trust me. Close your eyes and let it come."

"Derek—"

"Shh, you're doing great. Imagine you're just looking at a picture. It can't hurt you."

His voice steadied her as much as his touch. It was a tone she'd never heard him use before. Calm yet compelling, almost…professional. She didn't consider pulling away. He did make her feel safe, he always had. She relaxed against him, soaking in the strength of his body.

"Tell me your impressions." He skimmed his palms along her arms. "Don't think about it, just go with your gut. Say whatever comes into your head."

An image flickered on the edge of her vision. She tried to do what he said, but if she really went with what her instincts were telling her, she'd run the other way. "It's hot. The ground hurts my feet."

"What do you see?"

The scene flashed in front of her, as brief and stark as if it were lit by a bolt of lightning. For a split second, she saw the white tractor trailer lying on its side, gold bars scattered across the ground in jumbled heaps and gleaming in the sun so brightly they hurt her eyes…

The image winked out. Sighing, she wrapped her arms around Derek's waist and pressed her cheek to his shirt.

A white truck and gold. It was obvious what she'd just remembered. It was the accident after the gold heist. She'd known she'd been there. The police had told her.

Yet until now, she hadn't fully grasped the reality of what she'd lived through. As with everything else, there was a huge difference between reading about something and experiencing it in real life.

"Hey." Derek brushed a kiss on her hair. "Are you okay?"

She nodded. Derek was right: what had happened in the past couldn't hurt her now.

Besides, she should be pleased. As brief as the glimpse had been, this proved that she could remember.

"That wasn't so bad," she said. "Actually, considering how hard my subconscious tried to make me forget, I thought it would be worse."

* * *

Derek pinched the bridge of his nose, then rubbed his eyes with his thumb and forefinger. His eyelids felt like gravel, every muscle in his body was crying for sleep, yet his energy level was spiking just as it had in the old days, when a hunch was about to pay off and he was closing in on an arrest. Things were coming together, he could feel it.

He returned his gaze to the computer screen and clicked on the next image. Now that he knew where to look, he had been able to put a face to the man behind the Brotherhood. He studied Hart McAllister's mug shot from his most recent arrest. The photograph was over ten years old, but McAllister had the kind of lean features that likely wouldn't have changed significantly with age. His jaw was square, and no ounce of extra fat softened his sharp cheekbones. Beneath heavy brows, his dark eyes were set deep in their sockets.

The Colonel looked like a man who took good care of himself physically to the point of narcissism, probably as a way to compensate for the imperfection of his injured leg. He was looking straight at the camera, his expression calculating and slightly superior, which fit with his perception of himself as a commander. He hadn't yet established the Canyon Brotherhood when that photo had been taken, but the predisposition was there. Derek would bet McAllister went as far as wearing his old uniform when he dealt with his men.

Would McAllister have sent a new team to pursue Lydia, or would he have given the original three a second opportunity? There was no doubt in Derek's mind that someone was out there looking, in spite of the fact that no one had approached yet. The furor in the press over Lydia's disappearance would work in the Brotherhood's favor; with so many people looking for her, the team the Colonel sent wouldn't raise any suspicions when they nosed around.

Derek turned his head to check the alarm system was armed, then rolled his chair across the floor to the screen that monitored the closed circuit cameras, just to verify that everything was quiet. He didn't want to take chances with Lydia's safety.

Sure, but he was willing to help her dredge up the most traumatic event of her past. No, he'd done more than help her, he'd manipulated and encouraged her. Then he'd exploited the bond of trust they'd established in order to push her to go further.

Derek shoved himself to his feet and paced to the window, trying to ignore the jab of his conscience. He should be pleased about the progress she'd made today. His strategy was paying off—he'd gotten further with his low-key, relaxed approach in three days than those ham-handed Denver feds had managed in a month. From what Lydia had told him, she'd glimpsed the aftermath of the robbery. That was probably the worst of the memories and the hardest to face, yet she'd handled it well. It was only a small step, but now that she'd breached the block she'd put on those memories, the rest should come more easily.

What's more, the images of the gold robbery and the accident had probably been eating away at her subconscious her entire life. They might have been a contributing factor in her shyness and her preoccupation with safety. Her father should have gotten her therapy as a child so she could deal with them instead of suppressing them for his own ends.

So it was actually to Lydia's benefit that she take control of those memories.

Yet Derek still felt like crud.

He glared at his reflection in the window. He'd adjusted the glass to dark blue at sunset, and his face looked as hard and cold as a hunk of cobalt. She'd called him handsome, and she'd blushed at his teasing. How would she look at him when she learned the whole story? How would she feel about kissing him then?

He was digging himself a deeper hole every time he touched her, but the hell of it was, he couldn't stop. What was happening between them was gaining strength faster than he could have imagined. He'd been drawn to her from the start, and now that she was gaining confidence and opening up, he found her more fascinating than ever. She was blossoming before his eyes.

Yet she wasn't really changing, she was unwrapping what had been there to begin with, as if her decision to look for the gold was unlocking more than simply her memories.

The phone rang. Derek checked the time, then crossed the room to answer before the machine picked up. It was 1:00 a.m., so it was unlikely that this was a business call.

"Stone here," Derek said.

"It's September, Derek."

The voice was deceptively mild, like granite cloaked with velvet. Tony Monaco's voice was as distinctive as everything else about him. And time zones were meaningless to Tony, because there was no telling which one he would be in on any given day.

Derek's heart rate bumped up a notch. He wasn't surprised by the call—he'd known he would get it sooner or later. "I'm aware of the date, Tony."

"And I believe it was June when I asked you to repay my favor."

"I'm making progress," Derek said. "In the past week, the key aspects of my plan have come together."

"I'm pleased to hear it." There was a clink of crystal. Strains of a Tchaikovsky concerto played in the background. "You've been a valuable member of Payback, although I did have my reservations about bringing someone of your background into our network."

Tony was referring to the fact that Derek had worked in law enforcement. In most circumstances, that would have been considered an asset, but not to Tony or the majority of the members of this group.

"This is why your lack of results disappoints me," Tony continued. "Other men who lack your expertise have managed to fulfill their obligations in a fraction of the time I've allowed you."

"Other men weren't asked to bring down the Canyon Brotherhood."

A low, raspy laugh came through the receiver. "Ah, but Derek, anything less wouldn't have been a challenge to someone with your skills. Regrettably, I can't make exceptions, even for you."

Derek wasn't surprised by this, either. He'd known it was coming sooner or later, too. Yet that didn't prevent the dread. He tightened his grip on the receiver, his palms damp. "What's it going to be?"

"The helicopter."

Damn. He loved that bird. It wasn't vital to his tour business, he just enjoyed flying it. "When?"

"Two members of Payback will arrive tomorrow at noon. I trust you will make sure the transfer goes smoothly."

Derek replaced the receiver and wiped his palms on his jeans. This was how it began. One piece at a time, Tony would take back what was his. The helicopter was merely the first installment. The only way for Derek to keep from losing the rest was to complete the task Tony had given him.

So he should be pleased he was making progress with Lydia's memories, and to hell with the fact that this was hard on her. Changing course now wouldn't solve anything. He should be eager to wrap this up for both their sakes. Finding that gold was the only way either one of them would be able to get on with their lives.

He grasped the back of the swivel chair that sat beside the desk, his fingers whitening on the fabric. For a man who was normally in control of his emotions, he hadn't been doing a good job of it lately.

Why now? With all that was at stake, it was the worst possible time to confuse his priorities. And of all women, why did it have to be Lydia who stirred him?

He restrained himself for only five seconds before he gave in to his frustration and sent the chair spinning across the room.

It hit the shelf beneath the window with a satisfying crash. Yet the noise wasn't loud enough to drown out the gasp from the office doorway.

As if he had conjured her out of his guilty conscience, Lydia stood on the threshold, looking tiny and vulnerable. She was wearing her sneakers and one of her shapeless jogging suits. Her eyes were widened, magnified by her glasses, making her appear more like a frightened doe than ever.

Derek rubbed his face, trying to rein in his temper. "Sorry, if I startled you," he said.

She wasn't looking at the chair he'd shoved. She wasn't even looking at him. She was staring past him. Her breath rushed out as if she'd been punched. In the space of a heartbeat, the color drained from her face.

He glanced over his shoulder to follow her gaze. Hart McAllister's mug shot was still on his computer screen. Derek whipped his gaze back to Lydia.

She was moving her head in a slow negative, her gaze locked on McAllister's picture.

Derek crossed the room and took her hands. "Lydia, do you recognize that man?"

She kept shaking her head, but he had a feeling it wasn't to reply to his question, it was to deny what she saw. Her hands felt like ice, her chin was trembling and her gaze was filled with stark terror.

Possibilities burst through his mind. His gut had been right! There was a connection between McAllister and the gold. And whatever it was, Lydia must know. Even better, she was remembering.

This was what he'd wanted, wasn't it?

The hell it was. She was scared out of her wits. He moved sideways, blocking her view of the screen. "Lydia, it's only a picture," he said. "Nothing can hurt you here, I promise."

She snatched her hands from his and stumbled backward, her gaze fixed on something that only she was seeing. She bumped into the door frame, gasping for air. Then her eyes rolled back and her legs crumpled. She was already out cold before Derek caught her.

Chapter 7

Lydia's throat was raw, her ears ringing. She screamed to wake herself up, but the nightmare pulled her in deeper. She was looking at the monster, the embodiment of her every fear. Any child would recognize him. He was the wind that moaned outside the door, the shadow in the closet and the creaking floorboard in the dark. Until now, she hadn't realized he had a face.

But that was him. She felt it.

"Lydia, it's okay to wake up. You're safe."

She couldn't catch her breath. She couldn't scream loud enough.

"No one's going to hurt you."

She opened her eyes and saw a tall figure bending over her. She struck out in panic. Her fist connected with a solid chest.

Hands gripped her shoulders and gave her a gentle shake. "Lydia, look at me. It's Derek."

His voice finally penetrated her hysteria. She blinked, trying to bring her vision into focus.

"You're all right," he said. "You're in your room at my house. You're safe."

She still couldn't catch her breath. She arched her back, her lungs heaving.

Derek slipped his arm behind her shoulders and helped her to sit up. "Take it easy," he said. "Slow breaths. In and out."

"I saw…" Her teeth chattered. "I saw…"

He sat on the bed facing her, took her hand and placed it on his chest. "We'll do it together. Breathe like this," he said, inhaling.

Her hand rode his chest. She concentrated on matching his rhythm until the panic receded. She tried to focus on her surroundings, but the light was dim and her glasses were gone, the whole room was a blur. She turned her head, moving her gaze along her arm to where her fingers splayed on Derek's shirt.

"Is that better?"

She glanced down and saw that she was still dressed. She remembered she hadn't been able to sleep and she'd gone to Derek's office—

"Oh, my God," she muttered. "It wasn't a dream. That face was real."

"It was just a picture. He isn't here."

She closed her eyes, squeezing them hard enough to send patterns swirling across her eyelids. "I know he isn't. I'm sorry I hit you. My God. Did I faint?"

He stroked her forehead, brushing her curls back with his knuckles. "Yes."

"I don't understand it. I've never fainted before in my life."

"Something about that man frightened you."

The face threatened to return. She looked at Derek so it wouldn't come back. "Who is he?"

"We don't have to talk about it now. Just relax."

"How can I relax when I think I'm cracking up? Tell me who he is."

For a while it seemed as if he didn't want to answer her. "His name is Hart McAllister. He might have been involved with the gold robbery."

She shook her head fast. "If he was, I don't remember him. I don't know that name. I don't know who he is. I have no idea why I reacted..." It was getting hard to breathe again. She moved her hand over Derek's heart. She couldn't feel the beat through his shirt, but she could sense it. That, plus his breathing, pushed the panic back some more. "I was coming to get my clippings. I'd left them in your office. I couldn't sleep and I wanted to go over them again to see if I could remember more because that last one was so easy. Oh, God. I don't think I can. Not if that face—"

"Shh." Derek slid closer and looped his arms behind her back. "It's okay, Lydia. You don't have to do anything you don't want."

Don't cry, sweetheart. Daddy's coming soon.

Fragmented images tumbled through her mind, disconnected and confusing. A room with pink roses on the walls, little round lights over the bus seats, losing her shoes in the sand. The only common thread was the fear.

The nightmare was still there, lapping at the edges of her mind. Lydia curled into Derek's embrace, sheltering in his warmth. It was all right, he would keep her safe. The bogeyman couldn't find her here.

Bogeyman? It was a child's word. The thought made her want to laugh, but the sound that came from her throat was closer to hysteria than to humor. What on earth had she remembered?

You want the gold, not me.

The voice had seemed so real, Lydia lifted her head to look around. It had been a woman's voice. Her mother's? But her mother hadn't been present at the robbery. None of this made sense.

Lydia closed her eyes and leaned her forehead against Derek's shoulder, bracing herself in case there was more, but nothing else came. The only sounds she heard were Derek's steady breathing and her own pulse throbbing in her ears.

"Derek?"

"I'm right here."

She pressed closer. The need she felt for contact with a warm, living body was overwhelming. "Would you hold me, please?"

He shifted so that he sat farther back from the edge of the mattress and pulled her onto his lap. "How's this?" he asked.

She slipped her arms around his waist, grateful for his solid presence. "Thanks, Derek. I'm sorry to make such a fuss."

"Don't apologize, Lydia. This is my fault." He rubbed her back. "I'm the one who pushed you into dredging up your past."

"No, it was a good idea. It's just…" She paused, unsure how to explain and too shaken to make the effort. "I don't understand what happened. I'm not normally given to dramatics. Maybe I'm cracking up."

"Or maybe it's the middle of the night, you're exhausted because you've had a hell of a few days and you're just being human."

She locked her hands together over the side of his

ribs. He had done it again. How did he always know exactly what to say to make her feel better?

And how was it possible that they had met only a few days ago? Already she had shared more with him than with any other man in her life.

Then again, before this, she hadn't had much of a life, had she?

But at least she'd been safe. She hadn't heard voices or seen the face of a monster.

She trembled. She tried not to think about it, but the man's image flickered across her vision anyway. The dark eyes, the face like a knife. It wasn't gone, it was just…waiting.

If her memories of the gold were buried under that one, they might stay buried. She wasn't sure she wanted to dig around in there.

With a sob, she turned her face toward Derek's neck, nuzzling aside his collar with her nose. She drew in his scent, anchoring herself in the familiar sweet tang.

He swallowed. She could feel the motion against her forehead. "Lydia?"

She slid her hand up his shirt until her fingers brushed the top button. "I'm sorry, Derek. I'm not as brave as I thought I was."

"Don't be so hard on yourself. You'll feel better once you get some sleep."

"I don't want to sleep." She fumbled his button out of its hole and pressed her mouth to the triangle of skin that she'd bared.

He sucked in his breath through his teeth. She thought he might have sworn, but if he had, it was too low to hear.

Lydia felt the tickle of his chest hair against her chin and opened another button. The hair was crisp, springing back against her lips as she moved her mouth lower. The texture was at once soft and firm, incredibly masculine, filling her senses as thoroughly as his scent, mercifully leaving no room for anything else.

Derek moved his hand to her nape. "Are you okay?"

"No, I'm not," she whispered. "I'm not okay at all." She opened the rest of his buttons, parted his shirt and slid her palms inside.

His muscles contracted under her hands. "Lydia, what are you doing?"

Her fingers shook as she explored the dips and rises of his abdomen. She couldn't answer his question, because she had no idea what she was doing until her hands did it. "Derek, you feel so good. Just let me touch you for a while."

"I said I'd hold you, Lydia."

"Thank you." She followed the contours of his chest, tracing the pattern of his hair, savoring the way the texture grew silkier as she moved lower. She reached the hollow of his navel at the edge of his belt buckle and caressed it with the tip of her thumb.

He groaned.

Lydia slid her hands along his belt and around to his back. His skin was so warm, the heat spread through her palms and up her arms. Her sleeves bunched at her elbows, getting in the way. Without another thought, she pulled back, grasped the hem of her sweatshirt and yanked it off.

Derek moved fast, grabbing her wrists and trapping her hands inside the sweatshirt. "Lydia, you're upset."

Cool air wafted over her skin, yet it made her feel warmer. She wriggled her shoulders, and her nipples puckered against the satin cups of her bra. She whimpered at the sharp pleasure of the sensation.

"You're upset and rebounding," Derek said, his voice growing hoarse. "It's a natural reaction. The flight-or-fight response."

She heard what he said, and on some level, she knew he was right, but she didn't care. Oh, she longed to be touched on her breasts, but Derek's grip on her wrists hadn't loosened. Twisting, she managed to press only the side of one breast against his chest.

He shuddered, his entire body hardening. "You're doing this to run away from what scared you."

She shifted on his lap. Through layers of fleece and denim, she could feel his thighs flex beneath her buttocks and his erection swell against her hip. Her pulse soared. "Derek, let go of my wrists. Please."

"You're not thinking straight, Lydia."

"I'm doing this not to think. That's the whole idea." She arched her back, grazing her satin-covered nipple over his chest. "Oh," she sighed. "That's wonderful."

"I'm trying like hell not to be enough of a bastard to take advantage of you." He moved slowly from side to side, increasing the friction on her nipple. "But I'm not a saint, either."

"Don't you want me to touch you?"

"Damn it, you can feel for yourself that I do."

"Then why are you stopping me? You said you wouldn't."

"I don't want you to hate me."

"How could I hate you?"

"If we go any further, you might."

She leaned to kiss his neck. "If you say something about protecting me for my own good, I will."

"Lydia your first time shouldn't be like this."

She rubbed the edges of her teeth along a stiffened

tendon. The fact that he'd guessed didn't surprise her. "Then what should it be like?"

"I never thought things would go this far. We need to talk. There are things about me that you don't know."

"I don't care. I'm doing what you said. I'm going with what I feel. I'm trusting my instincts."

"Lydia—"

"I'm twenty-nine years old, Derek. How much longer am I supposed to wait to start living?"

His grip on her wrists tightened to the brink of pain.

Lydia moaned. The reminder of his strength didn't frighten her, it thrilled her. She could feel his restraint, and that thrilled her, too. With the tip of her tongue she traced the tendon up to his ear and closed her teeth around the lobe.

He released her wrists and threw her sweatshirt to the floor, then caught her head between his hands. "Last chance," he said, pulling back to look into her eyes. "Are you sure this is what you want?"

She'd never seen his gaze so intense. It snapped with emotions, with barely leashed desire. For a heartbeat she wanted to scurry away, to find someplace safe to hide and not make a sound.

Yet that urge was swept aside by a sensation of certainty. In that instant, she knew this was more than a natural reaction of her body. She didn't simply want contact, she wanted Derek.

She rubbed her cheek against his palm. "The only thing I'm sure about," she said, "is that I want you to be the one to show me."

His hands shook. He grasped her by the waist and lifted her off his lap. The next thing she knew, she was lying on her back in the center of the bed and Derek was on his knees, straddling her hips.

The intimacy of the position left her light-headed. The mattress dipped beneath their combined weight, another new sensation, having a large man sharing her space on a bed. She ran her hands over his knees and up his thighs, enjoying the hard warmth she could feel through the denim. "Was that a yes?" she asked.

He laughed. It was deep, rich and so sexy that the sound alone sent a pulse of pleasure zipping through her belly. He peeled off his shirt, then lowered himself on top of her, keeping most of his weight on his knees and elbows yet giving her the contact she craved. As gently as a whisper, he brushed his chest over her breasts.

Lydia bit her lip to keep from moaning aloud. Her bra felt too small.

Derek touched his tongue to her mouth. "Let it go, Lydia," he said. "I want to know what you like."

She arched her back. "That."

He slipped his hands beneath her and unfastened her bra. The friction of satin gave way to the rasp of chest hair and then, oh, he was using his lips. She couldn't have kept the next moan inside, even if she'd tried, so she didn't.

Derek smiled against her skin, laced his fingers through hers and moved her hands with his as he stroked her. "Feel what I feel," he said. "You're swelling into my touch."

She had a moment of shyness over the shared caress, but it quickly faded beneath the force of her response. She'd asked him to show her, and that's what he was doing. She just hadn't expected him to start by showing her her own breasts.

Yet it was exactly what she needed. With his hands guiding her, she explored places that she'd taken for granted. A curve here, a fold there, a tiny dip that he lingered to kiss.

It was more erotic than she could have dreamed.

"You're perfect," Derek murmured, releasing her hands as he slid downward. He ran his palms over her ribs to her waist, then followed with a trail of kisses. "Why would you want to hide this figure under fleece?"

She couldn't reply. Not only did she have no answer, her mind was reeling from yet another sensual assault. He was stripping away her jogging pants, his large hands moving slowly over her thighs to her knees.

"These are so sexy, I'm tempted to leave them on," he said, kissing the strip of satin that crossed her hip. He ran his tongue along the edge of her panties, then hooked his thumbs beneath the waistband and tugged them off. "But I've got more I want to show you."

And he did. Oh, how he did. He parted her knees, knelt between them and captured her hands once more, resuming their shared exploration. Every inch of her skin was so sensitized, she quivered with each touch. The more she wordlessly urged him to hurry, the more he seemed to savor the caress. By the time he dragged their joined fingers over the inside of her thigh, Lydia was trembling with the need for more.

She slipped her hand from his and lifted her hips from the mattress, her body throbbing. The pleasure was turning to strain. "Derek!"

He stretched out beside her and pulled her into his arms. Lydia hadn't realized he'd gotten rid of the rest of his clothes until his bare leg rubbed against hers. She angled closer and the firm length of his erection pressed against her thighs.

The reality of what was about to happen cut through the sensual spell Derek had woven. Lydia blinked and focused on his face.

He wasn't smiling. He looked hard, almost dangerous. Every angle and line was tight with need, the cost of his patience while he'd lavished her with attention.

Yet his beautiful lake-blue gaze was as naked as his body, shining with a plea that went straight to her soul. This was the man she had glimpsed before, the one beneath the charm. She couldn't possibly turn back now.

Lydia wasn't sure who moved first. Instinct took over, and the next move was so natural, she did it without thought. She had a moment's pain, but she'd expected that. What she hadn't expected was the feeling of completion, of total rightness. They did fit. It was more than physical.

She hooked her leg over his hip as he rolled her to her back. Each of the places he'd awakened with his touch pulsed with need. Time lost its meaning as he filled her, stretched her and made her writhe. And all the while he kept his mouth sealed to hers, joining them in a kiss that matched the rhythm of their hips.

There was no room left for thought or for fear as the first wave of bliss crashed through her. Lydia wrapped her arms around Derek and hung on, losing herself in the passion that she hadn't realized she had, trusting him to guide her back safely.

Lydia awoke to the sound of running water and tuneless whistling. There was no instant of confusion, no sleepiness to dim her thoughts. She knew immediately where she was. She stretched and rolled to her back, a smile already on her face. Sunshine was pouring through the skylight in the center of the bedroom ceiling, angling across the bed she and her lover had shared.

Her lover. Lydia bounced the term around in her mind for a while. It seemed far too sophisticated, a word that would be used by jaded women of the world who had affairs. She wasn't sure she was quite ready to call Derek that, although technically, that's what he was, regardless of how it had come about.

Her mind touched briefly on what had precipitated all of this, but quickly shied away.

She didn't want to think about how they had ended up together in her bedroom. Fear had no place amid the sunlight and twisted bedding that stretched across the mattress and spilled onto the floor. The terror was from her past. It belonged to some scared little girl, not to a woman who had finally become, well, a woman.

Tentatively, she moved her hand down her body, imagining the way it had felt when Derek had done it, then slid her hand across the sheet to the place where he had slept. She could still feel a trace of his heat. A piece of a condom wrapper lay on the corner of the mattress, and she blushed at the sight of it—apparently Tony had a standing order that every bedroom in his house be stocked with a good supply. The drawer in the bedside table where they'd been stored gaped open crookedly, mute evidence of how eager she and Derek had been. She grasped his pillow and hugged it to her chest, inhaling what remained of her lover's scent.

All right, she would think of him as her lover, even though neither of them had mentioned love.

But could this…glow she felt be only from sex? There must be more than a physical bond between her and Derek. Why else would he always seem so attuned to her needs? He was a sensitive, empathetic man. He'd realized all along why she'd wanted to make love. He'd even tried to be honorable and talk her out of it.

Yet he hadn't tried all that hard, she thought, pressing her face to his pillow. Once he'd decided to cooperate, he'd definitely been willing. And able. Magnificently able. Delightfully, tirelessly and insatiably able.

"Good morning, Lydia."

She turned toward his voice. She was pleased that he'd stayed to use her bathroom instead of leaving her to use his own. In spite of the lingering tenderness in certain places, she felt a reflexive contraction between her legs at the sight of him.

Oh, Lord, he was like a lonely woman's fantasy come to life. Tall and lean, he moved toward the bed with an easy grace, his muscles ridging subtly under his tanned skin. A turquoise towel from her bathroom was wrapped low around his hips, but the rest of him was gloriously bare. Moisture gleamed from the planes of his chest and his shoulders, and his hair was wet, slicked flat to his head.

She had a moment of awkwardness. Not having slept with a man before, she'd never had to deal with the proverbial morning after. She knew things wouldn't be the same between them, yet where should she start? She parted her lips, but she was unsure what to say.

He settled the issue by leaning one knee on the mattress, catching her chin in his hand and bending over to give her a kiss.

Derek tasted like mint mouthwash. It wasn't something Lydia would have thought was romantic, yet the ordinary, first-thing-in-the-morning taste somehow made the kiss more sensual. So did the drop of water that fell from his hair, landed on her shoulder and trickled down her breast.

She forgot about the awkwardness and tossed aside the pillow so she could grasp his shoulders. Without breaking the kiss, she angled her legs beneath her, got to her knees and moved across the mattress until she could press into him from thigh to chest.

She sighed as she felt his arms go around her. It had been dawn before they'd fallen asleep. She'd been sated to the point of grogginess, yet the passion was stirring again. For both of them.

In spite of what she could feel beneath his towel, Derek didn't take the kiss further. He eased his hips away from hers and moved his hands to her shoulders. He studied her face, his gaze troubled. "How are you feeling?"

She smiled. So that was the source of his hesitancy. He was concerned about her welfare. Of course, he always was. "Not that I have anything to compare this with, but all things considered, I probably feel better than I should."

"You're not sore?"

At the question, the region he referred to throbbed, a pleasant reminder. "I'd rather feel that than feel nothing. I have no regrets, Derek." She tried to read his expression. "Do you?"

He squeezed her shoulders, then straightened up from the bed. "Only that we didn't talk more first."

She grasped the edge of the sheet and wrapped it around herself as she got to her feet. "Derek, I'm sorry if you think I used you. I know I was upset, but—"

"You? Used *me?*"

"I realize I threw myself at you."

"Lydia, don't blame yourself. You were just reacting to your emotions. I knew what was happening."

"That's what I mean." Holding the sheet to her breasts with one hand, she tugged the other end free of the bed and moved toward Derek. "You were wonderful, but I was only thinking about myself."

A muscle in his jaw twitched. "You've got it wrong."

"No, I need to say this." She placed her hand on his

chest. "From the time you stopped to help me on the road, you've been doing nothing but giving. You gave me a place to stay, you're helping me straighten out my life, you're treating me like a normal woman instead of some repressed freak."

"Lydia, stop it. You're not a freak."

"Well, that's what I was until a few days ago."

He covered her hand with his. "You're an intelligent, fascinating woman. And if those scratches on my shoulders mean anything, you're sure as hell not repressed."

She glanced at the red streaks on his skin. "I'd forgotten about that."

"I'll never forget any of it. The sex we shared last night was the best I've ever had."

She leaned forward to kiss his knuckles. "Thank you for saying that, Derek."

"For God's sake, don't thank me! I mean every word of it."

She looked up. "Why are you angry?"

"Because what we did blew me away. One taste of you and I'm already hooked." He took her hand from his chest and stepped back. "But I can't think straight when you touch me."

"Is that a bad thing?"

"It is when all I want to do is unwrap that sheet and take you back to bed, but I can't, Lydia. Before we go any further, you deserve to know the truth."

She anchored a second hand in her sheet. Her fingertips were suddenly too cold to feel. "Are you married? Is that it? You said you didn't have a girlfriend, but you never mentioned a wife."

"Damn it, I'm not talking about us. What's between you and me is a hundred percent honest. I'm talking about the gold."

At the word, an image stole into her mind, a heap of tumbled bars.

You want the gold, not me.

And just like that, the nightmare was back, whirling across her vision in a choking cloud. Her feet hurt, her throat stung. She saw sand and gold. Her fists were caught in her mother's skirt and the bogeyman was coming. She watched his shoes. Dust stuck to the one that he dragged and oh, God, she didn't want to see what happened next....

Lydia couldn't help it. She ran.

Chapter 8

Lydia moved so fast, she was out the door while Derek was still absorbing the fact that she'd dropped the sheet. Any man would be distracted by all that skin. He'd seen everything there was to see last night, but admiring the perfection of her figure while she'd been lying in bed hadn't prepared him for the sight of that petite body jiggling in a full sprint.

He dropped his towel, grabbed his jeans and yanked them on. The jeans were for Lydia's sake. Judging by the distress on her face before she'd run, she wasn't trying to entice him. She likely hadn't even realized she was naked. And if she saw him giving chase in his current condition… "Lydia!" he called, pulling up the zipper as far as he dared. The stud would have to wait. "Lydia, stop!"

The corridor echoed with the soft slap of bare feet on stone. She didn't reply.

Derek snatched the blanket from the foot of the bed and ran after her. She was already at the bend of the corridor when he crossed the threshold. "Lydia!"

She was going so fast, she missed the bend and hit the wall with her shoulder. She scrambled to get her legs under her and pushed off with her palms.

Worry gave him speed he hadn't realized he had. He rounded the bend in time to see her cross the foyer and reach the outside door. "Lydia, I'm sorry," he called. "Please, give me a chance to explain."

She was trembling from head to foot, her hands wrapped around the brass knob that was set into the center of the door. She tried to open it, putting her shoulders into her efforts but he could see by the green light on the panel beside it that she hadn't thought to deactivate the electronic lock. She moaned, slapped the door with her hand and twisted to look over her shoulder.

He slowed, alarmed by the panic in her gaze. "Lydia," he said, trying to calm his voice. "It's too cold to go out like that."

"No!"

Her voice had the same thread of irrational terror he'd heard the night before. She wasn't trying to escape from him, Derek realized. She was running from a memory.

Was this the same memory that McAllister's picture had stirred up? Probably. Now that it had surfaced once, it would again.

She renewed her efforts to open the door, her head snapping back as she jerked at the handle.

"We're the only ones here, Lydia," Derek said, moving closer. "The door is locked. No one else can get in."

She kicked at the door with the side of her foot, then pivoted to face him and flattened her back against the wood. Her face was pale, her eyes huge. Her chest heaved as she struggled for air.

Derek kept his gaze on her face and his movements slow as he gestured to the corridor behind him. "Look, it's empty. No one's coming."

She pressed her hands to her mouth and looked past him.

"Tony has a zillion gizmos," he said. "Motion detectors, closed circuit cameras, all the latest toys. His security system is top of the line."

His words appeared to be having an effect. She blinked. Her eyes no longer seemed as glazed.

He smiled. "This place is safe, remember? You said that all it needs is a moat and it would be a castle."

She drew in a shaky breath through her fingers. "Oh, my God," she whispered. "I saw…" She shook her head. "No."

Derek could see the panic gradually ease from her expression. He wasn't sure how she would react if he touched her—he remembered the way she had struck out at him the night before—so he held out the blanket instead. "Whatever you saw, it can't hurt you now."

Still shaking her head, she focused on the blanket. It took a few more seconds before full awareness finally returned. She glanced down quickly, then stepped forward and grabbed the blanket from his hand. She flung it around her shoulders and held it closed at her chest.

He blew out his breath—he hadn't realized he'd been holding it. He should question her now, while the memory was still fresh, but he could see how hard she was struggling for control, so he wasn't going to push her. He pulled up a fold of the blanket and tucked it under her chin. "Lydia, it's okay."

"I must be cracking up."

"You remembered something again."

"I know that. But I don't understand why it feels so *real*."

He stroked her cheek. "You buried it deep. You never had a chance to deal with it before, so it's hitting you hard when it comes out."

"Well, it's coming out now, whether I want it to or not. I guess throwing myself at you again isn't going to help this time."

He wanted to argue. If she made the slightest move in his direction, he'd be all too willing to help her use him that way as much as she wanted and to hell with his conscience and doing what was right.

Her chin trembled. She tipped her head away from his caress. "My mother was there, Derek. With the gold."

He dropped his hand, trying not to be disappointed. "Your mother?"

"It was so clear, like a video clip instead of a snapshot. I remember she was wearing a black dress with a pattern of small white dots. We were both on the ground. I heard her voice." She tightened her grip on the blanket, her knuckles disappearing in the folds. "She was saying that he wanted the gold, not her."

"Who was she talking to?"

"The man…" She paused. "I saw something like this last night, but it wasn't as specific, and I didn't want to think about it. I just wanted to run away. My mother was afraid of him."

"Hart McAllister."

"The name doesn't mean anything to me. It's only his face I remember." She looked at Derek. "Why did you have his picture?"

"That's part of what we need to talk about." Derek held out his hand. "Let's go someplace where you'll be more comfortable."

She glanced at his hand but didn't take it. "No. I want to know now."

"It can wait. You're still upset."

"What else do you expect? Onc minute we're kissing, the next minute you're pushing me away and then this nightmare starts up again and—" She glanced around the foyer. "I don't understand any of this."

He cupped her shoulders. "I'm sorry, Lydia."

"You said I should know the truth about the gold." She shrugged off his touch. "Tell me now."

This wasn't how he'd envisioned telling her. He'd known the truth would have to come out eventually, and he'd hoped to break it to her gently to minimize her reaction. Yet delaying it was no longer an option. He'd realized this moment had been coming the instant he'd decided to sleep with her. That's why he'd brought up the subject first thing this morning.

But damn, he should at least have had the sense to wait until she'd put on some clothes.

"Derek?"

He turned aside to finish fastening his jeans, then paced across the floor while he tried to gather his thoughts. "When I told you about my debt to Tony Monaco," he said, "I didn't tell you everything."

She frowned. "What does Tony Monaco have to do with the gold? You said he wouldn't accept it."

"He wouldn't. I owe him more than money."

"I still don't understand."

"He kept me from going to prison and helped me get my life back on track. You can't put a dollar value on that, and he doesn't want money. I have to earn my way out of debt by bringing someone else who escaped the law to justice."

She leaned back against the door and looked around, her gaze moving over the priceless art that hung on the foyer walls. "I realize he's a wealthy eccentric, but I had no idea…"

"It's the same for everyone he helps. We all agree to repay his favor by evening the score. That's why he calls the group 'Payback.'"

"Payback?" she repeated. "Is that some kind of government agency?"

"Absolutely not. No one in authority knows the group exists. It's Tony's private justice crusade. He's righting wrongs one person at a time."

She took her hand from the blanket to rake her fingers through her hair. "That's all very admirable, but what does this have to do with the man in the picture?"

He returned to where she stood. "Three months ago, Tony selected an outlaw militia group that's known as the Canyon Brotherhood as the target for his justice. Since then, I've chipped away at it by setting up some of the members to be arrested by the cops, but I haven't been able to get near the man at the top."

She watched him in silence, her forehead knitted with confusion.

Derek pushed on. "Hart McAllister, the man whose picture you saw, is the leader of the Brotherhood. The cops only know him as the Colonel. Those three men who attacked you last week were sent by him because he wants the gold. That gold is his Achilles' heel. It's the best way to draw him out so the feds can arrest him."

"Wait a minute," she said. "I only told you about my father's gold last week, but this sounds as if you already knew that this man you're after is connected…" Her words trailed off. "You already knew."

There was no point softening this part. He nodded once. "It wasn't a coincidence that I was traveling the same road that you were. I've been watching over you since I discovered the Brotherhood was interested in you. I went down the Colca River a year ago. I wasn't in South America last month, I was in Denver."

"You were *watching* me?"

"The gold is the key to getting McAllister. Your memories hold the key to the gold. I had been waiting for a chance to approach you when you made a break for it."

"You lied from the very beginning!"

"Everything happened so fast, I went with my gut. You'd been put through hell because of that gold. I didn't know how you would react to the truth."

"Rescuing me, bringing me here, it was all a charade."

"Not all of it. I wanted to keep you safe."

"You wanted the gold all along."

"Not for me. I need it for bait to get McAllister, the Colonel. It's so I can pay my debt to Tony and—"

Her fist caught him square in the chin, knocking his head backward with a crack that echoed through the foyer. He hadn't seen it coming—he'd been concentrating on her face, not her hands.

He flexed his jaw. For a small woman, she had a mean right hook. Still, anger was a healthy reaction. He'd rather see that than see her retreat into her shell. "I deserved that."

She swept the excess length of the blanket from the floor, looped it over one arm and walked past him. "You played me for a fool, pretending you wanted to be my friend."

He followed her. "No, that was all true. I did try to be your friend."

"So you could talk me into finding the gold. And here I believed you were being helpful. You were only trying to help yourself."

"I won't deny that paying back Tony is my top priority, but so's your welfare."

"Sure."

"Think about it, Lydia." He stepped in front of her, forcing her to stop. "Recovering that gold really is the only way you're going to be free to get on with your life. I was able to talk you into it because it was the right decision."

She jabbed her finger at his chest. "Don't you dare say you lied to me for my own good."

"But I did. You weren't in any condition to listen to reason when I found you, and I didn't know you well enough then to guess how you'd react. To get rid of that block on your memory, I needed your cooperation."

"Oh, you got that, didn't you?" she said, her eyes shining. She jabbed him again. "You cooperated me right into bed. Was that part of the charade, too?"

He wrapped his arms around her, trapping her hands against his chest. She kicked at him, but she only got in a few solid hits before her feet got tangled in the blanket. He turned and backed her against the corridor wall, using his size to immobilize her. "The only thing I wasn't honest about was the gold."

She lifted her chin and glared at him, her cheeks flushed with color. "Let me go."

"Not until you hear me out. All the things I told you about myself were true. I'm the same man I was five minutes ago, and you seemed to like me well enough then."

"Derek…"

"Everything that has happened between us was real."

"Why should I believe you?"

He parted the blanket with his knee and pressed his leg between hers. "Because you felt it, too. I showed you."

She shuddered. "The sex was nice, but as I said before, I have nothing to compare it to. For all I know, it's always like that."

He lifted her in his arms, braced his knee against the wall and pulled her forward so that she straddled his thigh. "It isn't."

She twisted, trying to free her hands from the blanket, but her movements drove her more firmly against his leg. She bit her lip, her pupils expanding.

"Go ahead and hate me," he said. "I warned you that you would. But don't ever doubt that the passion we shared was genuine."

"Put me down."

"I'm not done yet."

Her thighs tightened around his leg. "You should have told me the truth."

"If I had, would you have let me touch you?"

"No."

He flexed his thigh, rocking her gently on his leg. "Are you sure?"

"Stop that," she murmured.

"You know the truth and the sparks are still there. I can feel your heat through my jeans."

"If you're trying to prove that my body responds to yours, you've made your point. Now let me go."

"Is that what you really want?"

"You duped me and you used me. I might be new to this sex stuff, but I'm not desperate enough to sleep with you again."

He lowered his knee gradually, letting her slide down his body until her feet touched the floor. Before he released her, he put his lips next to her ear. "I know I should apologize for taking your virginity, Lydia, but that's the one thing I'm not sorry about." He flicked her earlobe with the tip of his tongue. "I'm glad I was the one to show you how to fly."

Lydia stuffed the last sock into her gym bag and looked around the bedroom. She hadn't made the bed. The sheets were as she'd left them. So was the towel Derek had dropped. They looked different now that the patch of sunshine from the skylight had progressed from the mattress to the floor. Dimmer. Tarnished.

She moved her gaze to the painting across from the bed. The nude's smile no longer looked mocking. It glowed with a sad wisdom. Welcome to womanhood, she seemed to say. Isn't it a bitch?

Lydia tipped up her glasses to wipe her eyes. She wasn't sure why she was crying. She'd known that what had happened between her and Derek had only been sex. It was what she'd wanted from that first tickle of excitement when she'd seen him standing in the rain and smiling that dangerous grin.

So he'd lied to her. It wasn't the first time a man had lied to her, was it? Her father had lied, and lied well for her entire life. She resented his lies. Her grief when she thought of him was tangled with anger. Yet that didn't change the fact that she loved him.

Good thing that there was no love involved with Derek, wasn't it? It was a crush, infatuation. Lust. She'd used his body to escape her fears.

He'd pulled her strings like a master puppeteer. God, how could she have been so gullible? In hindsight, it was perfectly obvious how he'd manipulated her into doing what he'd wanted, but she'd been too flattered by his attention to scrutinize his motives. She'd been swept up in a romantic fantasy of her own making, wild with her first real taste of freedom.

And okay, she'd admit it, she *had* thought that what had passed between them had been more than simply sex. They might have known each other for only a few days, yet her feelings had been rapidly deepening. Otherwise, she wouldn't have slept with him no matter how distraught she'd been.

But he hadn't wanted her, he'd wanted the gold.

The words were too familiar. Was the gold cursed? Was that why she felt sick whenever she thought of it? Had something similar happened to her mother?

A wisp of the nightmare brushed her mind. Lydia sat on the corner of the bed, folded her hands over her stomach and waited in dread, but nothing more came. Still, she could taste the fear on the back of her throat. Whatever had happened to her mother, it had been far more serious than a romance gone sour. Rose had been terrified of this McAllister person. Why? And why had he been there with the gold? Where had Lydia's father been?

There were so many unanswered questions. The more she remembered, the more she realized she didn't know. She had to find out the truth, if not for the gold then for her own peace of mind.

Think about it, Lydia. Recovering that gold really is the only way you're going to be free to get on with your life.

Moaning, she dropped her head into her hands. It was likely that Derek had been trying to pull her strings again when he'd said that. Yet in spite of her injured pride, she had cooled off enough now to admit that he'd been right. The gold would always be a problem. As long as it was out there, she would run the risk of being the target of someone like McAllister. Or Benjamin. Or Derek.

Finding that lost bullion and giving it back to the government still was the only reliable long-term solution, no matter what else it stirred up. Lydia wasn't going to give up on that. But as far as Derek went...

She returned her gaze to the painting. There was strength in that woman's sad but knowing smile. She had probably had so many excellent lovers she'd lost track of her first. If she happened to run into him on the street someday, they would likely greet each other like old friends and share cappuccinos at some sidewalk café in the best worldly, sophisticated fashion.

But Lydia wasn't there yet. She could understand Derek's deception and rationalize all she liked, yet it still hurt. Yes, he'd shown her how to fly, but in her heart, she was still foolish and naive enough to wish that the trip could have lasted longer. She put on her jacket and hooked the strap of her gym bag over her shoulder, then picked up her purse and left the bedroom.

She had no trouble with the front door this time—it was unlocked when she reached it. Derek was standing outside, his back to the house. His jacket collar was turned up and his hands were shoved deep into his pockets, as if he were bracing himself against a cold wind. Yet the boughs of the fir trees that rose from the top of the ridge were barely moving, and the midday sun was warm. At the sound of the door, he twisted to look over his shoulder.

For a moment, his gaze was unguarded, and the turmoil she saw there stunned her. This was how he'd looked in the instant before they'd made love the first time. No smile, no charm, no defenses whatsoever. He looked totally alone. And in spite of everything that had passed between them, she wanted to run to him and take him into her arms.

A hawk cried from the valley beyond the cliff's edge, and the moment passed. Derek's gaze dropped to the bag she was carrying, and his expression closed. "Going somewhere?" he asked.

She shut the door behind her and walked to where he stood. "Yes. I'd like to go to Durango if it's not too much trouble."

The breeze stirred the ends of his hair, bringing her the scent of shampoo, and she thought about how his hair had looked this morning when it had been wet, and how the water that had dripped from the ends had felt like a caress.

"Why?" he asked. "Are you giving up on the gold?"

She closed her hand around the strap of her gym bag. "No, I'm not giving up, but you don't seriously expect me to stay here now, do you?" she asked.

"I hoped you would. You thought it was a good idea before. Nothing has really changed."

"Maybe not for you, but it has for me. I would find it much too awkward to continue our association under the present circumstances."

He took his hand from his pocket and ran his fingertips along her temple. "You're a smart woman, Lydia. You've got every right to resent the way I finessed you into looking for the gold, but you wouldn't have gone along with me unless you believed it was a good idea."

"You duped me."

"That was my fault. I made a snap decision and ended up underestimating you. I apologize for that."

It was so much easier when she could be angry with him. It helped her remember why she shouldn't trust him. He was far too good at saying what she wanted to hear. She stepped back and he dropped his hand. "If you don't want to give me a ride, I'll walk."

"Lydia, you don't have to do that. I brought you here, and I'll take you wherever you want to go, but I wish you'd reconsider. What do you plan to do in town? The Brotherhood thugs took your money," he reminded her. "You only have thirty dollars and ninety-five cents."

"I'll get a job. I'll manage somehow."

"You have bigger concerns than money. McAllister wants that gold, and he knows as well as I do that you hold the key to finding it. If you go to town, someone might recognize you, and that could bring out the treasure hunters and the Brotherhood. You'd be safer here."

She hooked her purse strap over her elbow, thrust her fingers into her hair and grasped a handful of curls. "I don't look like my picture anymore. I'll take the chance."

He tilted his head to study her. "You're right. You don't look much like you used to, but it's not only your hair that's different. You're looking more...you." He paused. "But it's dangerous for you to leave here with no protection just because you want to prove something."

"What do you mean?"

"That's why you want to leave, isn't it? You want to prove that you don't need my help because you're still annoyed at me."

"Annoyed is putting it mildly."

"And it's your pattern to avoid what upsets you."

"My pattern?"

"I thought you were starting to change that."

He was doing it again, she realized. Subtly guiding her to the path he wanted her to take. "You missed your calling, Derek. You should have gone into psychology instead of computer programming. I'm sure you would have been a very successful shrink."

A shadow crossed his face, a twinge of pain that he was unable to hide. "I wasn't a computer programmer, Lydia."

She dropped her gym bag and backed away, holding up her palms. "You mean there's *more* you haven't told me? Why did you lie about that?"

"I didn't lie. You assumed I worked with computers, and I let you believe that because I didn't want to explain the truth."

"Why not? And don't tell me you wanted to protect me, because I'm sick to death of hearing it."

He reached out to her, but she took another quick step backward and bumped against one of the wrought iron benches that sat in front of the house. She windmilled her arms to keep her balance, jerking aside when he tried to help.

He closed his hand into a fist and dropped it to his side. "No, Lydia. I was protecting myself. I didn't want to talk about my old life because I put it behind me when I met Tony. I'm not proud of the way I left it."

"Your old life…" She paused. "Did you lie about having an honest job? Were you a criminal before you robbed Tony's store? Is that it?"

"No, it's the opposite. I was a cop."

The hawk screeched again from the valley. The cry was farther away this time, yet the noise made Lydia jump. Derek kept his gaze steady on hers, his jaw tensed as he waited for her reaction.

The details began to click, small things that Lydia

hadn't put together before but like everything else, they seemed obvious now. There were Derek's fighting skills, his criticism of how the Denver police had dealt with her, his ability to access confidential databases, his analytical mind, his professional tone…

And the haunted look on his face when he'd spoken about his honor.

"I worked for the Denver FBI," he said. "I was a profiler, so your guess was close to the mark. I have a background in psychology."

She knew what profilers did. They were the experts who analyzed suspects through their behavior patterns and figured out the best way to manipulate them, to *finesse* them, as Derek had done to her.

God, this was worse than she'd thought. She'd believed he was simply an insightful and sensitive man, but it was no accident that he'd always seemed to know the right thing to say. No special bond between them had been involved. He'd only been doing what he'd been trained to do.

She slipped past him, scooped up her bag and walked toward the long, low building that served as the garage. "Just when I think it's over, I find out I'm an even bigger fool than I thought I was."

"Lydia, no."

"Then what was I? Some kind of psychological case study? A specimen to analyze?"

He fell into step beside her. "Never, Lydia."

"Of course, I suppose I couldn't have been much of a challenge to crack compared to the hard-boiled suspects you usually dealt with. There wouldn't be too many lonely, twenty-nine-year-old virgins on the FBI's most-wanted list." She reached the square pillar that held the control panel for the garage door and smacked the top with her palm. "Open it, Derek. Give me your keys and I'll drive myself."

He grabbed her hand and held it next to his face. "Want to hit me again? Would that help?"

"You're the professional. Why don't you tell me?"

"There's nothing remotely professional about what happened between us. In all my years with the bureau, I never got emotionally involved with a case. That's why I was so successful. No one got to me, until I met you." He kissed her palm. "I care about you, Lydia. If I didn't, I would have kept going the way we were and wouldn't have told you anything."

She was pathetic. All he had to do was touch her and she started to melt. "That's just the right tone of contrition. Mentioning caring is an effective ploy, too. You must have been very good at your job."

"I used to be the best," he said. "But right now I have no idea what it would take for you to stay."

"I suppose trying the truth never occurred to you?"

"The truth is that I've followed a hunch and dug myself into a hole. I was betting everything on using the connection between McAllister and the gold to pay my debt to Tony and now I'm running out of time. You're my last chance. If I don't keep my promise to Tony, the life I've built for the past seven years will mean nothing."

He sounded so sincere. Was he really opening up to her, or was he just pulling her strings again?

The old Lydia would have bought this immediately. She would have remembered how vulnerable Derek had looked when he'd talked about having burned his bridges. She might have thought about how well-suited he'd seemed to the business that had helped him turn his life around. Then she'd feel all warm with sympathy and think of what a sensitive man he was and the next thing she knew she'd be caught up in that infatuation again and pretending it was more.

He laced his fingers with hers. "I need you, Lydia. I don't want you to leave."

I love you, baby. Remember that. I don't want to leave you.

She dropped her bag and drew in her breath, her mother's voice echoing in her mind. How many times had she heard her now?

And she'd been an idiot to think about love. The only honest thing between her and Derek had been the sex.

"Lydia, are you all right?" he asked, leaning closer. "Was it another memory?"

Damn it! Was this what he wanted? Was he playing her again, deliberately getting her emotional in order to stir up her memories?

She hated these doubts, but she'd be a fool not to consider them. Maybe that was what her mother's voice was trying to warn her about. There were parallels between the present and the past. She snatched her hand from his. "Don't touch me, Derek."

"Lydia—"

"Just leave me alone. That's what you wanted anyway, isn't it?"

"What's that supposed to mean?"

"You knew from the start this—what did you call it?—this *enjoyment* between us wouldn't last. Don't pretend to care now. It's too late."

He looked the same way as he had when she'd punched him.

The urge to take him in her arms was stronger than ever, but it wasn't only Derek she couldn't trust. She didn't dare trust her own feelings.

Before he could reply, a car horn sounded from the direction of the gates. She turned to look and saw sunshine glint from a windshield.

Derek jammed his hands into his jacket pockets as he moved beside her. "Great," he muttered. "They're right on time."

A sleek black sedan drove through the gates and moved along the driveway, bringing with it the rumbling purr of a powerful engine. It stopped midway to the house and a tall, dark-haired woman in a sky-blue jumpsuit emerged from the passenger side. She blew a kiss to the driver, then jogged toward the flat landing area on the leeward side of the ridge where Derek kept his helicopter.

Lydia could sense the tension in Derek's body, even though he stood a foot away. He might have expected these visitors, but he wasn't pleased about them. It must have been why he'd been standing outside. Was that also why he'd looked so lost when she'd first seen him? "Derek?" Lydia asked. "What's going on?"

"I told you I'm running out of time," he said. "Tony's repossessing the chopper."

"What? Can he do that?"

"He can do whatever he wants. He made the rules, and I agreed to play by them."

The car continued toward the house until it rolled to a stop in front of Lydia and Derek. The driver's door opened. A man dressed completely in black got out and stood in the V of the open door. He was wearing leather driving gloves and designer sunglasses, the picture of elegance from his neat dark hair to his polished shoes. "Derek," he said.

Derek remained where he was, not offering his hand or moving forward to greet him. "Lydia, this is John Kipling," he said. "He's another member of Payback."

John arched one eyebrow as he glanced at her gym bag. Otherwise, his face remained expressionless. "Hello, Lydia."

Whether she trusted Derek or not, she was grateful for the reassurance of his presence. Although John Kipling appeared slender rather than musclebound and he dressed like a gentleman, he exuded an aura of leashed power that bordered on sinister.

"Tony hadn't told me it would be you, John," Derek said.

"I was in the neighborhood anyway." John rested his elbow on the top of the car door. "And Tony has a way of expressing himself so it's difficult to refuse."

A low whine rose in the air. It echoed from the house and the garage, gradually increasing in pitch.

Derek squinted as he looked toward the helicopter. "Who's the pilot?"

"New recruit. She joined a month ago, so Tony's giving her a taste to keep her motivated."

"Yeah, that's Tony. Never misses a trick." The sound of the helicopter engine moved into a steady chug. "I hope she knows what she's doing. That bird has its quirks."

"Seeing as how it's Tony's bird now," John said, "she'll be guarding it with her life."

Through the thin screen of trees, Lydia could see the main rotor begin to turn. It moved sluggishly at first, slowly gaining speed until she could no longer distinguish the blades. Dust stirred by the downdraft whirled along the cliff top. The noise level continued to rise until the helicopter lifted smoothly into the air, did a quarter turn to the left and flew off.

Derek waited until the drone had faded, then swore softly and widened his stance, as if he were once more bracing himself against a cold wind.

"Sorry, Derek," John said. "It's nothing personal, just business."

"Yeah, I know. Any idea what it's going to be next?"

"The house. He's giving you two more weeks."

The *house?* Lydia thought. Would Tony really evict Derek from his home because he hadn't paid his debt?

"Damn," Derek muttered.

"After what happened this morning," John said, "you've got to understand that Tony's pissed."

She started, looking from Derek to John. Tony couldn't possibly know what was going on between her and Derek, could he? And what business of his would it be, anyway?

"What are you talking about?" Derek asked.

John took off his sunglasses and regarded him somberly. "I take it you haven't seen the news today."

"No, we've been busy. What's going on?"

"It appears the Brotherhood has just declared war."

Chapter 9

Lydia wanted to look away from the horror on the screen, but she couldn't. The ambulances, the fire trucks, the smoke, all of it evoked memories of horror, yet these memories weren't uniquely hers. The aftermath of a bombing was familiar to everyone these days. It was a tragic fact of life. The location could change, so could the scale of the destruction, but the images of suffering were universal and once seen were never forgotten.

"Initial reports confirm that eleven people are dead and thirty-five are missing. The count of injured stands at twenty, but these numbers continue to change as rescue personnel work their way through the debris." It was the same announcer who had been anchoring CNN two days ago. She had been all but snickering when she'd read the story about Lydia's disappearance. She was dead sober now. "The blast was centered in the surgical wing of the hospital complex, but the long-term care facilities have also received heavy damage."

Derek held his cell phone to his ear as he paced in front of the living room window. His body was as hard as the sound of his boots on the wood floor. "Come on," he muttered. "Pick up the damn phone."

The grim report continued. "The authorities haven't released any details of the nature of the explosives used, but eyewitnesses reported seeing an ambulance parked near the blast site shortly before the explosion. Other Amarillo area hospitals are being overwhelmed as the evacuation of patients continues."

Lydia undid her jacket and slipped it off without taking her eyes from the screen. The view switched to a shot from a news chopper, revealing a sprawling complex with white walls and a red-brown roof surrounded by parking lots with treed boulevards. It should have looked peaceful. Instead, it looked like a war zone. "A hospital," she murmured, moving her head back and forth in disbelief. "What kind of monsters would bomb a veteran's hospital?"

But as the announcer's next words revealed, there was no mystery as to who was responsible. "A militia group calling itself the Canyon Brotherhood has claimed responsibility," she said. "In a handwritten manifesto delivered to a local radio station, they claim a long list of grievances against the American government and vow to strike again."

Footage of a fireman carrying a white-haired man in a bloodstained hospital gown rolled across the screen. Paramedics jogged behind gurneys with more injured. Pieces of paper and plaster dust mixed with the smoke that billowed from a ragged hole in the side of the five-story building in the background. The view switched to a reporter who stood amid the chaos. He was visibly shaken, his voice difficult to hear above the sirens and the screams. People jostled past him, some fleeing the scene, others rushing in to help.

The anchorwoman returned, giving an updated estimate of casualties. A phone number scrolled past beneath her, an information hotline for patients' relatives.

Derek closed his phone, went to the stairs that led to the upper floor and took them two at a time. "I'll be in my office," he said.

Lydia dropped her jacket on the couch and followed him. She'd left the rest of her belongings in the foyer beside the front door, the ride to town forgotten.

Leaving no longer seemed as pressing an issue. Her personal feelings were trivial in the face of what had happened. How could she be concerned about herself when innocent people had been killed?

Derek was already seated at his computer by the time she reached his office. The same knife-sharp face from her nightmare was on the screen. She faltered, grasping the door frame.

Let us go. I'm begging you. You want the gold, not me.

You're mine, Rose. You can't disappear this time. There's no place to hide.

The voices flickered between one heartbeat and the next and were gone as quickly as they'd arisen. Lydia breathed deeply, pressing her forehead to the door frame. After lying dormant for most of her life, her memories were suddenly ambushing her.

Was there a reason she was remembering certain things, or were they merely random firings of her synapses?

"Lydia, are you all right?"

She pushed upright and moved into the room. "I'm fine. What are you doing?"

Derek closed the file with McAllister's picture and typed in a few lines of code. "I'm sending the information I have on McAllister to the FBI."

She glanced around the office, suddenly remembering what John Kipling had said about Tony taking the house. There was so much going on, it was difficult to absorb it all. "Will that pay your debt to Tony?"

"No, but it might save lives." He tapped some more buttons. A progress bar started working across the screen. "I should have sent it sooner."

"Is that who you were trying to call? The FBI?"

He spun his chair away from the computer and got to his feet, as if he were too agitated to remain seated. "I was trying to reach my old supervisor. We didn't part on the best terms, but she's the smartest agent I know. The authorities need to be made aware of the details behind McAllister's grudge against the government and the military. He's likely going to continue choosing targets that symbolize his personal grievances."

She had never seen him so tense before. Whether or not he'd been playing her before they'd come inside, this was no act. She didn't believe for a second that he was putting on his distress over the bombing as a ploy to manipulate her emotions. "How would a veteran's hospital be a symbol?" she asked.

"Hart McAllister was wounded in Vietnam and spent almost a year at the hospital in Amarillo that was just bombed. He never fully recovered, and he likely holds them partly responsible." He walked to the shelf beneath the window and picked up his climbing axe. "Damn, I should have warned someone."

"Have the Canyon Brotherhood done anything like this before?"

"No, they've been keeping their activities low-key. It's probably because they've been raising funds to build up their strength."

"Then how could you have predicted they would do this?"

He ran a fingertip along the curve of the axe blade. "I had a gut feeling they were planning something big, but I sat on the information because I didn't want the feds interfering with my own plans too soon."

"Derek, you can't blame yourself for this tragedy."

"I should have found some other way to nail McAllister. I wasted too much time—"

"On me."

He tossed the tool back on the shelf and focused on her. "On a hunch. A long shot."

She had a crazy desire to apologize, but she didn't know what for. She hadn't asked him to include her in his convoluted scheme. It wasn't her fault that he'd run out of time to pay his debt and was about to lose his home. And she wasn't responsible for those deaths in Amarillo any more than he was.

Still, she was involved in this now. "It wasn't that much of a long shot," she said. "The man in my nightmare had trouble walking. I remember sand sticking to his shoe because he dragged his foot."

"McAllister's left leg was shattered by an artillery barrage."

"Then it must be the same man, and he is connected to the gold somehow and to my mother. She was terrified of him. I have a memory of riding on a bus at night. I think she might have been running from him."

Derek nodded. "He's got an obsessive personality. If

he was involved with your mother, he probably wouldn't have let her go easily."

"When I first saw him, all I could think of…" She hesitated, then said the word anyway. "He was the bogeyman. I must have grown up being afraid of him, but I don't know how he would have been connected to my mother."

"You said your mother was a nurse."

"That's right."

"Amarillo isn't that far from Albuquerque. If your mother worked at the veteran's hospital during the late sixties when McAllister was there, it's possible he developed an attachment to her."

Lydia rubbed her arms. She felt as if something cold had brushed her skin. "But that would have been more than a decade before the bullion robbery."

"Like I said, he probably wouldn't have let her go easily. If he found her again when she was with your father, he might have gotten involved in your father's plans."

"However it came about, he was definitely there when the truck carrying the gold crashed."

"He might have been there, but something prevented him from taking the gold for himself. Otherwise, he would have used it instead of being in and out of prison on minor charges. He wouldn't have sent his men to question your father and then you."

She clamped her jaw briefly, fighting to keep her teeth from chattering. More horrors were stirring in the back of her mind. "You were right, Derek," she said. "He wanted the gold then and he wants it now."

Derek returned to the computer, checked that the progress bar tracking the transfer of his files was complete, then walked to Lydia. For a moment it seemed as if he were about to take her by the shoulders as he'd so often—and naturally—done before, but he pulled back before he touched her and folded his arms over his chest. "If McAllister and the Brotherhood manage to get their hands on the bullion, they could follow through on that threat in their press release and fund a wave of bombings worse than the one that happened in Amarillo this morning."

"I realize that."

"They have to be stopped."

"Yes."

"Is that why you're still here? Did you change your mind about helping me?"

He must have been a formidable agent when he'd worked for the FBI, Lydia thought. Determined, intelligent and not afraid to take chances. His gaze snapped with passion, a different kind of passion than she'd seen the night before, yet no less powerful.

It was little wonder he looked haunted at times. He'd worked in law enforcement, and he'd been driven to commit a crime. He'd betrayed the trust the bureau had had in him. In spite of the circumstances, Lydia felt a rush of sympathy.

No! she told herself. Things were already complicated enough, she wasn't going to let her emotions cloud her thinking again. "First, tell me how your plan would work," she said. "How would you use the gold to draw out McAllister so he could be arrested?"

"Simply put, it's bait. I plan to embed tracking devices in the bullion, then use my Payback connections to put out the word quietly that some treasure hunter stumbled onto it. When McAllister sends someone to acquire it, as I'm certain he'll feel compelled to do, I'll let them take it. The gold would lead the authorities straight to the Brotherhood's new headquarters."

"Do you really need to find the gold for that? Couldn't you bluff him with fake gold?"

"Whoever he sent would be certain to check that it was the real thing before they delivered it, so it couldn't be faked. In addition, the fact that it's real would put it above suspicion. He'd never suspect a tail because no government agency would risk that much gold."

"That's why you didn't want to involve the authorities."

"Right. I know how they operate. They'd never take a chance this big with government property. Once McAllister has the gold, I'll bring in the FBI."

"But will possession of that bullion be enough to put him in jail?"

"Now that the Brotherhood has gone public, there would be no shortage of grounds to arrest McAllister and the rest. It's only a matter of finding them." He stepped closer, still not touching her, yet near enough for her to feel the heat from his body. "I still believe in my gut that the gold is McAllister's weakness, and that theory is supported by everything you're remembering."

"Yes, it is."

"It's your call, Lydia. What do you want to do?"

The knife-sharp face blinked through her mind. The bogeyman. She wanted to run.

It's your pattern to avoid what upsets you.

She straightened her glasses on her nose and lifted her chin. "Right now, I want to stop the Brotherhood from killing anyone else, and if digging up my memories will help, then that's what I'll do."

"Thank you."

His voice had dropped to a low rasp, stroking her nerves, reminding her of how he'd sounded in bed. Her gaze fell on the gap at the open collar of his shirt, and she thought of how the skin she could see there had felt under her lips....

She curled her nails into her palms. "Fine. As long as we're straight about us, Derek."

He looked at her mouth. "Us?"

"We might share the same goal, but that's all we share. Our personal relationship is over. As soon as I figure out where my father hid the bullion, I'll want that ride to town."

The fire crackled on the hearth, blending with the sound of the music that played softly from the hidden speakers. Warmth and the homey scent of woodsmoke curled through the living room. Sunset tinted the thin clouds on the horizon with spectacular bands of color and cast a mellow orange glow on Lydia's face as she looked down on the valley.

Derek set the wineglasses on the table in front of the couch and assessed the atmosphere critically. The music was light rock because it was Lydia's favorite. The bottle of wine he'd selected from Tony's cellar was a California chablis, again because it was Lydia's preference. Everything had been chosen with her comfort in mind. He wanted to put her at ease so that they could explore her memories in a low-stress, controlled fashion.

But this looked more as if he'd set the scene for seducing a lover than for questioning a subject.

Of course, the seduction option wasn't likely to happen. He rubbed his chin, feeling a twinge from the place where Lydia had punched him. She'd made her feelings crystal clear. Once this hunt for McAllister and the gold was over, she wanted nothing more to do with him.

She turned away from the window. She had her arms crossed and her chin angled upward. Even if she hadn't spelled things out for him earlier, her body language alone was plainly telling him to keep his distance.

He knew that would be smartest. He had to stay focused. As John had warned him, Tony was indeed pissed, and his patience with Derek was running out. As of twenty minutes ago, the official death toll from the Amarillo VA hospital had reached thirty-one. Stopping McAllister and the Brotherhood before they struck again was imperative.

So no matter how much he wanted to go over there, haul Lydia against him and kiss that tension from her face, he had to act like the professional he used to be. Letting his personal feelings get involved any further could blow the only chance he had left.

"What do you want me to do?" Lydia asked.

No shortage of answers sprang to his mind, but few concerned the reason they were here. "That's up to you, Lydia. Where would you be the most comfortable?"

She moved to the couch and curled into one corner. "Don't you need a pendant or a watch on a chain to dangle?"

He opened the wine, poured two glasses and held one out to her. He waited until she took a sip, then carried his glass to the opposite end of the couch and sat on the arm. "I was a profiler, not a shrink, so my training didn't include hypnosis. That's not what we're going to do. We're just putting your mind into a relaxed state so your consciousness can flow freely. How's your wine?"

She gulped a mouthful and swallowed fast. "Great."

Derek regarded her with concern. "You need to loosen up, Lydia. You've been wired all day."

"What do you expect? I see the news, and I've been staring at those newspaper clippings and the picture of

McAllister, but nothing happens. I'm not even getting hints of my mother's voice anymore."

"It's not going to come if you try to force it."

She looked at him over her glass. "You told me that before, but I hadn't realized that you'd known what you were talking about."

"Whether you believe it or not, it's a relief to be able to tell you the truth."

"Well, it's certainly more expedient if you don't need to hide your expertise."

"Expertise isn't going to help if you don't loosen up and trust me."

"It's hard to do, Derek."

"I realize you'd rather be anywhere else but here. You were willing to take a chance on running into the Brotherhood as long as you didn't have to be around me. I got the message."

She studied him as she took another drink.

"But regardless of what you think of me, we both want the gold found and McAllister behind bars," he said. "That's one thing you *can* trust."

Some of the stiffness eased from her shoulders. "You're right."

"Why don't you try stretching out?" he suggested. "It might help."

She put her glass on the table, toed off her sneakers and shifted sideways on the couch.

He leaned over to lift up her feet, then slid from the couch arm to the cushion and set her feet on his lap.

She jerked. "Derek—"

"Don't worry," he said, laying his hand over her ankles to hold her in place. "I've got too much riding on this to let my libido get the better of me. Besides, I'm only touching your feet, so it doesn't count."

"Why are you doing that?"

"To help you relax." He set his untouched glass on the table and curled his fingers over her toes. He squeezed gently.

"Was foot massage one of your usual interview techniques?"

"Not really." He pressed his thumb to the ball of her foot. "It wouldn't have gone over too well with the guys on the FBI's Most Wanted list."

Her lips twitched. It wasn't much, but it was the first hint of a smile she'd allowed since the morning.

Derek forced himself to keep his touch casual. Sure, he was only touching her feet, and there was no more than a sliver of skin showing between the cuff of her sock and the bottom of her sweats, but after restraining himself all day, this contact was affecting him faster than wine.

Focus! he reminded himself.

"Let's start with something you already remember," he said. "Tell me about your father. What was he like when you were a kid?"

"He was much the same as when I was older. A stickler for rules and respectability. Shy, quiet and fond of cardigans. Except for his glasses, he was a regular Mr. Rogers."

Her words were flip, but her tone wasn't. He could hear the deep emotion behind it. "You miss him."

"Of course, I miss him. I loved him."

"In spite of his lies."

"They don't wipe out all those years of caring. He's the same man he was before."

He wondered if she realized how she'd just echoed what he'd said to her this morning. Part of him wanted to pursue it, to take advantage of the opening, but mending his relationship with Lydia—or even having one—wasn't his priority right now.

All along, he'd known their association would be only temporary. If he was successful and the Colonel and the Brotherhood were arrested, Derek would go back to traveling the world, looking for his next thrill. If he wasn't successful, he would be without a home, without an income and on the run from a loan shark. Either way, he had no place in his life for a woman.

"What's your earliest memory of the house where you lived in Denver?" he asked.

"It's a jumble of memories. I remember the smell of leaves on the ground and frost on the window beside my bed."

"Sounds cozy."

"It was. It always felt safe." She slid farther down on the couch so that she could rest her head on the arm. "I'm starting to understand why my father was so protective. He must have known that McAllister was out there. He'd be more of a threat than the police."

Derek rubbed her instep. "I've been thinking about that, Lydia. Seeing yourself with short hair is what triggered the first memory of your mother, right?"

"Yes, her hair looked and felt like mine."

"The fact that your father lied about your looks had been bothering me, since he hadn't otherwise been cruel, but I think I figured it out. Zachary must have noticed how much you were growing up to resemble your mother, and he probably wanted to discourage you from realizing how beautiful you actually were."

She lifted her foot from his lap. "Derek—"

"No, wait. Let me finish. I'm not trying to flatter you, I'm being practical."

"How's that?"

He cupped her heel and placed it on his thigh. "I think we can assume that McAllister was stalking your mother. When your father saw that you were growing up to look like her, he could have been worried something similar would happen to you, and that's why he tried to keep you close to home."

She blinked. "Oh, good Lord."

"What?"

"That article in the *Nugget* on the bookstore had both our pictures. I had assumed it was my father's picture that started all of this, but what if it was mine? What if McAllister saw me and recognized my mother?"

"He could have recognized both of you." Derek traced the ridge of her anklebone with his thumb and moved his fingers to her calf. "Your father might have been trying to hide you as much as himself."

"Well, that certainly helps explain why he wanted us to live the way we did."

"And why he encouraged you to camouflage your looks."

"That makes sense."

"Yeah, but it doesn't make it any less of a crime." His fingertips brushed the bare skin above her sock. "You have great legs, Lydia."

"Are you saying that to relax me?"

"Nope. I'm saying that because it's the truth. I'd bet you'd be a knockout in a tight skirt and high heels."

"I've never tried either."

"You'll have to add that to your to-do list."

Her lips curved again. "Maybe I will."

"Tell me about your mother's black dress with the polka dots."

"It was soft. It must have been cotton…." She sucked in her breath. "That was too easy."

"Keep going," Derek said. "Say whatever comes into your mind. What do you hear around you?"

"My mother's crying." She closed her eyes. "No, she's yelling."

"Is she angry?"

"She's scared. She's telling me to hide but I don't want to go because my shoes fell off when the truck crashed and the ground hurts my feet. Oh God, Derek. I'm seeing it again."

He'd had her almost relaxed, but he could sense her body stiffening with tension. In spite of the soft music, the wine and the firelight, there was no way to dull the impact of what she was remembering. And he had an insane impulse to tell her to stop.

Yet that wouldn't help her. She was bound to remember eventually, and he didn't want her to face it alone. He shifted closer, sliding her legs over his until he could take her hand. "Think of it as a picture. Just like you did before. I won't let anything hurt you."

Lydia clasped Derek's hand, grateful that he hadn't listened to her demand not to touch her. In spite of her confused feelings toward him, she needed the reassurance of physical contact to anchor her. She breathed deeply a few times, trying to keep the gathering panic from driving away the memory.

She *wanted* to see this, she reminded herself. The memory had been pushing at the threshold of her consciousness, waiting to be released for days. She wasn't going to run from it again.

Lydia curled forward, holding Derek's hand to her chest. "My mother's sitting on the ground," she said. "The wind's blowing her skirt as she's dragging herself backward."

Derek wrapped his arm firmly around her shoulders. "She must have been hurt when the truck crashed."

"Yes. I remember pulling on her arm to try and make her stand up, but she lost her shoes, too. They're black. I can see one of them."

"Is your father there?"

"No, but we're not alone...."

Fear rose like a haze of dust in the air. The man with the limp was coming faster than Lydia's mother could drag herself away. He had blood on his face that glistened as he smiled.

"You love me, Rose. I know you do."

"You're sick. Can't you see that? I was only doing my job."

"No, you belong to me."

"Zachary won't give up. He's going to find us. He'll be here any minute."

"You shouldn't have let him touch you, Rose." He lifted his hand. He was holding a gold bar. "Is this how he bought you?"

Lydia sobbed and locked her arms around her mother's neck. "You're mean! You hit Daddy. Go away!"

"Shut that brat up!"

"Shh, baby. Be quiet like a mouse now. Daddy's coming and everything will—"

The man brought down his hand. The gold bar struck the side of Lydia's arm but her mother twisted at the last second so that her own shoulder bore the brunt of the blow. There was a dull crack and her mother moaned.

Lydia's vision blurred with tears. She curled into a ball, holding her arm to her chest while the voices continued to scream through her head.

"You bastard. Don't hurt her!"

"Then you better do what I say."

"Let us go." Her mother lurched away from Lydia to clutch the man's shoe. *"I'm begging you. You want the gold, not me."*

"You're mine, Rose. You can't disappear this time. There's no place to hide."

"It's a fortune. More money than you dreamed of."

"It's for our future, Rose. That's why I wanted it. You're my dream."

"But you only asked for the gold. Zachary did what you said, now keep your word and let us go. Please."

"The brat can stay but you're coming with me."

"Even if I could walk, I wouldn't go anywhere with you. I love Zachary. I always will."

"You love me." He leaned over her and fabric ripped. *"I'll prove it to you."*

"No, for the love of God, don't—" She screamed. *"Lydia, run!"*

The gold bar flashed again. Her mother toppled to her side.

Lydia ran, her eyes streaming, her feet stinging. She ran until she couldn't breathe, then fell to her knees and crawled behind a heap of round boulders. She squeezed her eyes shut and put her hands over her ears, but she could still see and hear…

The memory snuffed out. Lydia didn't try to bring it back. She knew she wouldn't forget it again.

Her mother wouldn't let her.

Chapter 10

"Absolutely not." Derek gripped her arms and brought his face so close to hers it blurred. "I won't let you do this. We're going to use the gold for bait, not you."

"Hart McAllister stalked and kidnapped my mother," Lydia said. "He coerced my father into stealing that truckload of gold, then knocked him out and kept the ransom. I might have seen it all from a child's perspective, but it's not hard to figure out how the pieces fit together. He killed her when she was hurt and defenseless. He sent the men who caused my father's fatal heart attack. He destroyed my family, and I want him stopped now. I don't want to waste time with more memories."

"Think, Lydia! Your plan is too risky."

"I've had a lifetime of safety. It's all so obvious to me now why I lived through my books, why I never took chances and why I never flew." She twisted out of his grip and flung out her arm. Her hand hit the living room window but she barely noticed the sting of pain. She looked at the mountains that stretched across the horizon. The sunlit ridges were mottled by the shadows of fast-moving clouds, echoing the passage of her own emotions.

The previous night had been a blur. Remembering the violence that had ended her mother's life had left Lydia scoured raw. Derek had held her while the aftermath of what she'd seen had ebbed, then had helped her into bed and had sat with her until she'd fallen asleep.

"Look out there, Derek," she said. "It's a whole world I've been hiding from."

"You had good reason."

"Not anymore. I ran away like a scared little mouse and did nothing while a monster raped and murdered my mother. I had the knowledge in here all along—" she smacked the heel of her hand against her temple "—but I was too afraid to face it."

"You were five years old. If you had tried to help her, you probably would have been killed, too. You couldn't have done anything."

"I'm not five years old now. I'm a grown woman." She moved her hand to her breast. Instead of beige fleece, she wore one of Derek's company T-shirts. It was an extra-small size. Thin black cotton clung to her curves, revealing the figure she'd always concealed. "Now I finally understand why I was afraid of accepting it."

Compassion shone from his gaze. "Those scars from what you witnessed have to be deep, Lydia. I wish I could help you."

"You did. You didn't even know that you had." The sex they had shared had been healthy and natural. Without either of them realizing it, what they had done had been the best therapy possible.

She knew that McAllister's assault on her mother hadn't been about sex, it had been a twisted expression of control. Yet the buried memory of it had festered, robbing Lydia of what should have been a normal part of her life. She felt angry. Cheated. "Everything's so clear. This is the real reason why I became a lonely spinster who liked beige and wore her hair in a bun. It's why I was content to stay home and take care of my father."

"Your father wanted to protect you."

"Sure, but he didn't make me this way, *I* did. I've been living in fear because of what McAllister did to my mother. That's why she kept coming back to me, Derek. She wanted me to remember. She wanted me set free." She slid her hand down her midriff to her stomach. "And there's no mystery anymore why the thought of gold makes me sick. I saw her blood on the bars."

"He'll pay, Lydia. I'll make sure of it."

"So will I. That's why I'm going to lead the FBI to whatever rock he's hiding under."

"This is still too fresh for you," Derek said. "Give yourself some time to let it settle."

"It had twenty-four years to settle. I'm not going to avoid it anymore."

"I shouldn't have said you have a pattern of avoidance. I didn't know the whole story."

"No, you were right. Brilliant, in fact. You must have been an awesome FBI agent."

He flattened his hands against the window on either side of her, caging her between his arms. "I almost wish I still was one so I could slap a pair of cuffs on you and lock you up until you come to your senses."

She could see the tension in his face, and she could feel it in the heat that rolled off his body, yet she wasn't afraid. Even before she'd purged that terror from her past, she hadn't feared Derek.

She steepled her fingers on his chest. "Remember how you said my father made a mental prison for himself and brought me up to share it? Well, he couldn't have done it if I hadn't let him. No one's locking me up again, no matter how good their intentions might be."

"Why won't you listen to reason?"

"Why are you arguing with me? We want the same thing, and this is the fastest way to get it."

"It's too dangerous."

"That's a strange statement, coming from you. I thought you thrived on risk."

"Managed risk. Calculated danger. I won't take chances when it comes to your life."

"That's the operative word. *My* life. Nothing's holding me back now. I'm free to do what I want, and if I choose to use myself for bait—"

"Damn it, Lydia. I won't let you simply walk out there and offer yourself like some sacrificial lamb."

"Think like a profiler, Derek. McAllister's obsessed with the gold and believes I can get it for him. The Brotherhood's already looking for me. All I need to do is let them catch me. They won't suspect a trap."

"No."

"Those tracking devices you were going to use on the gold would work just as well on me. I'll lead the authorities straight to McAllister. It's simple."

"It's suicide."

"He wants me to tell him where the gold is. He won't kill me as long as he believes I know. That should give the FBI plenty of time to move in and arrest him."

"Too many things could go wrong. You could be caught in a crossfire." A muscle jumped in his jaw. "Or seeing your resemblance to your mother could push McAllister over the edge."

Some of her bravado faded. She saw the limping man with the bloody face, the gold bar raised like a club...

And for one cowardly, shameful instant she wanted to hide again and never come out, go back to her old self and how things used to be.

But her mother had protected Lydia until her last breath. How could she possibly let the monster who had killed her go free?

She met Derek's gaze. "We want to push McAllister's buttons. That's the whole point. We need to get him."

"Not like this."

"You can't stop me, Derek. The only question is whether or not you want to help me."

"Give the memories another chance."

"I don't remember what happened to the gold."

"Not yet, but you will."

"There's no guarantee, and I don't want to wait."

"I want to keep you safe."

"For how long? In two weeks you're going to lose this house."

A muscle in his cheek jumped. "You don't have to remind me what's at stake if I don't pay my debt to Tony."

"Once I leave here, the Brotherhood might find me anyway."

"I won't let that happen. I'll protect you."

"Again, for how long? Until McAllister has his men blow up another target?"

"Lydia—"

"I'm not staying with you indefinitely, Derek. We

were clear about that from the start. You're not responsible for me. You're not my keeper."

He regarded her in silence. Tension built, spinning out between them as her words hung in the air. When he finally spoke, his voice was rough. "Then what am I, Lydia?"

My lover.

The reply in her head caught her off guard. "As long as we're working together to stop the Brotherhood, we should consider ourselves partners."

He took one hand from the window and ran his thumb along the edge of her jaw. "Is that all?"

She shuddered at the contact. Her senses flooded with the scent of Derek's soap, his aftershave and the warm musk from his skin.

He moved his thumb to her mouth. Holding her gaze, he traced her lower lip. "If you want me to stop, say the word and I will."

The emotional turmoil that had propelled her through the morning suddenly flipped into a surge of sexual awareness. It didn't frighten her, it empowered her. This was normal and healthy. It was a natural extension of their impassioned conversation. The mere fact that she could feel it was a victory over McAllister.

"I won't pretend, Derek," she said. "I think we've come beyond that. It always feels good when you touch me."

He eased the tip of his thumb into her mouth, then drew it out slowly and moistened her lip with a smooth, gentle sweep. "What if I kiss you?"

She tilted her head to follow his caress. "It would feel good, too, but I'm not going to forget about my plan just because you kiss me."

"I know you wouldn't, Lydia."

"And a kiss isn't going to change anything between us, either. I can't forget that you played me for a fool."

"I know that, too." He took off her glasses and ran his palm down her arm. "So, can I kiss you?"

She realized this was crazy. Nothing had been resolved. Her pride wanted her to keep protesting, but the rest of her was aching to lose herself in the pleasure she knew that he could give her.

She hadn't replied aloud, but he must have read her indecision. Without another word, he brought his mouth down on hers.

The delight stunned her. It was immediate, slamming through nerves that were already sparking. She parted her lips, welcoming the bold thrust of his tongue, her body awakening with demands he'd taught her. After the remembered horror from the night before, this was more healing than anger. It was exactly what she needed.

She pulled back to look at him. Was he really this in tune with her, or was this just more evidence of his psychological expertise? She'd once thought they had a bond. She'd been naive enough to hope it might have been love. With everything else that had been going on, she hadn't taken the time to consider it again.

Yet she couldn't deny there was something special between them. He might have lied, but his actions hadn't. All along he'd been showing her what kind of man he was. The compassion wasn't a pose. His strength wasn't an act.

What *did* she feel?

He smiled, grasped her hands and stretched them over her head. He pressed her wrists to the glass, pulling her upward as he angled his hips against hers.

The frankness of his arousal made her knees buckle. She moaned and hooked her legs around his waist to keep from falling. "It feels as if you want more than a kiss, Derek."

"Yeah." He brought her hands to his shoulders so he could slide his arms around her back. With her held securely in his embrace, he turned away from the window and started across the room.

Oh, she couldn't think anymore. Whether he was playing her or not, she wanted this. She nudged aside his collar and pressed a kiss to his neck.

He reached the staircase, braced one foot on the second step from the bottom and stopped to settle her weight on his thigh. Grasping her hips, he shifted her until her body aligned perfectly with his.

Heat pooled between her legs, just as it had the last time he'd held her like this. There was no doubt he knew how to make her body respond. She undid his shirt buttons, pushed the edges aside and pressed closer. "I said I wasn't going to sleep with you again."

A low laugh rumbled through his chest, tingling across her hardened nipples. He rubbed the edge of his teeth along her neck. "It's the middle of the day, Lydia." He leaned forward with her and slid her off his leg to sit on a higher step, then knelt, parted her knees and nuzzled the inside of her thigh. "I'm not planning to sleep."

Even through the fleece, she could feel the warmth of his breath. She trembled, leaning back against the riser above her. The very staircase seemed to be shaking. She moved her fingers through his hair, remembering how good it had felt sliding across her thigh.

He tossed her sneakers over his shoulder, then hooked his thumbs into the waistband of her jogging pants and tugged them down her hips. A quick shift from one side to the other and he had them past her ankles. Within seconds all that was left from her waist down was a scrap of white lace.

Lydia ran the sole of her foot along his back, bunching his shirt under her bare sole. Her heart was thudding so hard, she felt giddy.

Derek kissed the inside of her knee as he moved his palms along her thighs. He was a scant inch from the top when his hands stilled. Lifting his head, he twisted to look behind him. "What the hell?"

She felt the vibration along her spine seconds before she heard the engine. Dazed, she looked past Derek's shoulders to the windows that stretched across the front of the living room.

Sunshine flashed from glass. A helicopter was coming in fast across the valley. The noise resolved into a rhythmic thump, gaining in volume as the aircraft swooped toward the house.

The mood shattered. Reality returned in a rush. Lydia pulled her foot from Derek's back and groped for her pants. Before she could reach them, Derek grabbed her hand and pulled her to her feet. "Go to your bedroom and lock the door. I'll find out what's going on."

She caught the banister and stayed where she was. Later she would probably be grateful for the interruption, but right now her body was throbbing with frustration. "I know who it is, Derek."

"Who?"

She pointed to the window. The helicopter banked as it neared the cliff top, revealing large white letters on the underside. Even without her glasses, Lydia was able to guess what they were.

He swore and whipped his gaze back to her. His shirt

gaped open, his chest was still rising and falling with his rapid breathing, but the desire that had warmed his eyes moments before was gone. "The FBI? What are they doing here?"

"I invited them."

"You brought the FBI to *Tony Monaco's* house?"

She snatched her pants from the staircase and jerked them on. "I told you that I'm not going to hide anymore, Derek. I'm going ahead with my plan to stop Hart McAllister, whether you help me or not."

The passage of seven years hadn't mellowed Special Agent Sandra Templar, Derek decided. A tweed suit, sensible pumps and a briefcase were her fashion statement. There was more gray in her hair, but her movements were as brisk and no-nonsense as he remembered. She'd been known as the Saint, not only because her personal life was as bland as one's, but because her reputation had been spotless and her ethics above reproach. She lived for her job, and she was damn good at it.

The last time Derek had seen her, he'd been cleaning out his desk. She'd made no effort to hide her disappointment in him—she'd taken his disgrace personally. She'd been his mentor when he'd joined the bureau, and she'd been the one to fire him.

Yet she hadn't come here to see him, she'd come to see Lydia. Lydia had used the redial on Derek's cell phone to call her.

"I see you've done well for yourself, Derek," Sandra said as she opened her briefcase. She drew out a laptop computer and set it on the dining table in front of her. "Are you enjoying the tour business?"

"It pays the rent."

"You have an interesting choice of landlord."

He crossed his arms and leaned back in his chair. He'd barely had time to turn off the countermeasures in Tony's security system before the helicopter had landed. Sandra had been the only passenger. The pilot was waiting outside, no doubt snooping around the perimeter on her orders. "Tony's an interesting man."

"Yes, so I've heard. I'm surprised you're associating with him."

The disappointment was still there in her voice. Like everyone else in law enforcement, Sandra was familiar with Tony's less than savory reputation, but she knew nothing about Payback, and Derek wasn't at liberty to enlighten her. "I'm surprised you got here so fast. I thought you were working out of the Chicago office now."

"I had business in Denver. I was on my way there when I received your e-mail." She flipped up the lid of her laptop. "You've obviously been doing more than conducting tours. The information you sent me yesterday has proved invaluable."

"I thought you'd know the right people to send it to."

"How did you happen to acquire it?"

"Old habits die hard."

He'd meant it as an offhand response, but she regarded him intently. "Yes, they do. Have you ever considered returning to the bureau?"

Her question caught him by surprise, not simply because she asked it but because of how he reacted. He felt a spark of energy, just as he had in the old days when a case had come together.

But that was history. He'd burned that particular bridge, hadn't he? "I'm just a private citizen now," he said, "doing my civic duty."

"Derek's being modest," Lydia said, carrying a tray with a tea service to the table. As she had since their visitor had arrived, she avoided looking directly at him. She appeared to be doing her best to act as if she was unaffected by what had been about to happen between them, but her cheeks still bore a telltale flush and the teacups were rattling in their saucers. She took a chair to Sandra's right, across from Derek, and passed a cup of tea to the FBI agent. "His skills as a profiler are very impressive."

"They always were." She nodded her thanks to Lydia for the tea as she clicked open some files. "The trouble was, he wasn't a team player."

"I've noticed," Lydia said. "He does like to keep his cards close to his chest."

"Ladies, I'm right here."

Sandra continued as if he hadn't spoken. "Take his investigation of the Brotherhood and McAllister. I'm sure he's not going to explain to me why he's involved, yet he would expect to use my resources regardless. For him, the end justifies the means."

"Yes, I've noticed that, too," Lydia said. "I hadn't realized that was a pattern with him."

"Unfortunately, it was. His insights were brilliant, but he had an issue with trust."

Derek rapped his knuckles against the table. "You didn't come all this way to discuss my faults, Sandra."

"That's true. I came here to meet with Miss Smith." She turned her chair toward Lydia, her posture signaling she was getting down to business. "After your call this morning I requested a check of the Amarillo Veterans Hospital personnel records. Fortunately, most of the old records escaped damage because they had been archived in a wing separate from the blast, so the agents on site were able to access them quickly." She paused to click through some files on her laptop. "A nurse by the name of Rose Dawson was employed on the surgical ward during the period Hart McAllister was a patient. Further checking with the local authorities turned up a series of restraining orders that she later filed against McAllister."

Derek sat forward. "Who else knows about this?"

Sandra regarded him coolly. "My people know how to be discreet, and I trust them one hundred percent. Otherwise, they wouldn't work for me."

"Rose Dawson must have been my mother," Lydia said.

"Yes, coupled with what you remember, I would have to agree." Sandra rotated the laptop so that the screen faced toward Lydia. "Her photo ID card was still in her file. The resemblance is remarkable."

Lydia's eyes widened. She pressed her fingers to her mouth.

Derek surged to his feet and rounded the table, concerned Lydia might react badly. Sandra shouldn't have sprung it on her that way. After what Lydia had gone through the night before, she didn't deserve to be ambushed.

But after her initial surprised gasp, Lydia regained her control and regarded the screen steadily. Her chin lifted with the same determination that had been evident since she'd awakened this morning. "That's her," she said. "That's my mother. I remember her smile."

Derek put his hand on the back of Lydia's chair and leaned over to study the photo on the laptop. The woman did look like Lydia, only her hair was red, and her features were accentuated by makeup and didn't seem as delicate. Still, the resemblance would have been enough to allow McAllister to recognize Lydia's picture in the newspaper.

"My colleagues at the Denver office were concerned with your safety, Miss Smith," Sandra said. "They had also surmised that the Canyon Brotherhood had been behind the attack on your father, but they hadn't been aware of the full extent of the connection, since there were so many other treasure seekers who descended on the area."

"The Brotherhood almost got her," Derek said. "The Denver guys dropped the ball."

Sandra's lips tightened. "That may be, but in light of the Amarillo bombing, time is of the essence, so I'd prefer not to waste it on reprimands. We need to capitalize on this information before more lives are lost."

"I agree," Lydia said. "That's why I called you."

"And I appreciate your courage, Miss Smith. This could be the break we need. McAllister doesn't know we've made the connection between him and your family, so he won't be expecting a trap."

Derek fisted his hand. "Sandra, you can't be considering going along with Lydia's plan to use herself as bait."

"Normally I don't like involving civilians in an investigation, but with the proper safeguards, it could work. You should know that."

He did. In the old days, he wouldn't have had any trouble putting aside his emotions and considering this logically.

But there was nothing logical about his feelings for Lydia. An hour ago they'd been arguing, thirty minutes ago they'd been on the verge of having sex on the staircase, and both activities had seemed perfectly natural.

She was turning out to be a hell of a woman. Not only

wasn't she timid, she had a spine of stainless steel. "There's no changing your mind?" he asked.

"No. I have to do this, Derek."

He met Sandra's gaze. "Then I'd like to help."

She dipped her chin in acknowledgment. "I've always respected your insights. If you have some suggestions, I'd be willing to hear them."

"McAllister wants the gold. It's his weakness. He wants to settle the score with that chapter of his life the same way he's using the Canyon Brotherhood to settle the score with the government."

"Agreed."

"So instead of Lydia, let's give him the gold. That's what he really wants."

Sandra raised her eyebrows, looking from Derek to Lydia. "Have you located it?"

"No we haven't," Lydia replied. "Derek, we've gone over this already. I'm not going to wait—"

"You don't have to. We'll call a press conference and have you announce that you've found Zack's lost gold. Say it's in safekeeping and make a big deal of how you're going to give it back to its rightful owner, the U.S. government. That's sure to push McAllister's buttons, not only because he hates the government but because he believes the gold is rightfully his."

Sandra drummed her nails against her keyboard. "Explain how this will work."

"I guarantee that someone from the Brotherhood will show up at that news conference. We won't let them get to Lydia, but we can let them get away with samples of the gold. As long as we rig the bars with tracking devices, even if the Brotherhood ditch whatever tail you put on them, the gold should lead you straight to the Colonel."

Lydia twisted to look up at him. "You told me you'd need to use the whole amount or they'd get suspicious."

"The whole amount would be better, but as long as you're convincing enough on camera, McAllister will believe you found it. That's all that matters. We have to hope his obsession with getting it outweighs his caution."

"But fake bars won't work. McAllister's men will test them."

"They're not going to be fake."

Sandra spoke up. "Derek, the bureau can't provide genuine bullion for a sting."

"Leave that to me," Derek said. "I know someone who can."

Chapter 11

Lydia stepped aside as a pair of men in suits hurried toward the front door. After almost a week of being alone with Derek, it was jarring to have other people in the house. Yet since Special Agent Templar had arrived the day before, the place had become the command post for what could have been a military operation.

She followed the voices toward Derek's office. He was standing in front of the bulletin board with Sandra Templar and a tall, raven-haired man she hadn't seen before. The stranger appeared to be pointing out routes on a high scale road map to two more FBI agents. The snapshots from On the Edge Tours that had covered the bulletin board were gone. In their place were duty rosters, lists of phone numbers and a floor plan of the Durango hotel where the press conference would take place.

The sight of it all sent a burst of adrenaline through

Lydia's blood. Events were continuing to progress at breathtaking speed. At times it was hard to believe she was really part of it.

Derek glanced over his shoulder, his lips parting as he caught sight of her. "Whoa," he murmured.

The gleam in his eye set off another punch of excitement. They hadn't been alone since yesterday, and their conversation had been limited to the sting they were planning. Neither of them had alluded to that...incident on the stairs, yet the sexual tension between them showed no signs of fading. All it took was a glance and her heart began to pound. She moved her hand to her hair. "Is it too red?"

Sandra turned to look at her, then crossed the room to study her critically. "It's perfect. The precise shade from Rose's picture."

"I hadn't realized how easy this was," Lydia said. "I've never tried dyeing my hair before."

"It's only a rinse. It should wash out in a few months."

Lydia nodded. The hair color had been Sandra's idea—she'd wanted to play up Lydia's resemblance to Rose for the cameras to push McAllister's buttons. "I don't mind," she said. "Actually, I kind of like it."

Derek rubbed his face, then squeezed his jaw as he looked at her. "Where'd you get the outfit, Lydia?"

"I picked that out while I was in town," Sandra said, answering for her. "I believe it will have the right effect, don't you think?"

"If you want to attract attention," Derek said, "that'll do it."

Lydia smoothed the dress over her thighs, warmed by the note of masculine appreciation in his voice. The dress was prettier than anything she owned—a simple, feminine design with a fitted waist and a short, flared skirt that ended at mid-thigh—yet they both knew she hadn't worn this to entice him. The only reason Sandra had bought it was because the fabric was black with small white polka dots.

"You look great," Derek said, touching her sleeve. "But are you okay with dressing like this? If it's too much for you, just let us know."

She shook her head. Derek had steadfastly objected to this aspect of the plan, and had argued with Sandra about it at length. His objections hadn't been professional—he'd been more concerned with Lydia's feelings than with pushing McAllister's buttons.

The horror of what she had witnessed as a child hadn't disappeared, yet it was losing its power to hurt her. Each time the memory swept through, it left her feeling stronger and more determined. "It's sad to be exploiting something so tragic," she said, "but I feel as if it's a tribute, too. My mother would probably want me to do it."

"How are the shoes?" Sandra asked. "You seemed to have trouble walking."

Lydia glanced down at the black heels that completed the outfit. Although they weren't as chunky as the eighties style she'd described to Sandra, they were close. "They fit okay, but I'm accustomed to flats. These are going to take some practice."

"You'll only need to walk as far as the microphone." Sandra moved to the briefcase she'd left on Derek's desk and withdrew her cell phone. "It looks as if everything's set. I'm going to schedule the press conference for tonight."

She started. "So soon?"

"We'll be ready." Sandra thumbed through her directory, then put the phone to her ear.

"Now that we've got all the props," Derek said, "there's no reason to delay."

"Props," Lydia repeated, pinching a fold of her skirt between her fingers. "I guess you mean this?"

"Not quite." Derek nodded toward the stranger. The black-haired man had apparently finished advising the agents on the map and came forward to greet her. "Meet Nathan Beliveau," Derek said. "He's volunteered to provide us with the backdrop for the cameras."

The stranger quirked one eyebrow. "Volunteered?"

"He's also good with road maps," Derek said. "Seeing as how he's in the trucking business."

Nathan shook Lydia's hand. "Your boyfriend can be very persuasive."

Lydia regarded him curiously. Unlike the business-suited FBI agents who had been coming and going all day, Nathan Beliveau wore a battered black leather jacket over a plain white dress shirt and black jeans. He looked more like a biker than a truck driver. It took her a moment to register his remark. "It's true, Derek can be persuasive," she said. "But he isn't my boyfriend. What backdrop?"

"Nathan brought a dozen ten-kilo gold bars," Derek said. "Sandra's techs are drilling them to install the tracking devices."

"Ten *kilo* bars?" Lydia exclaimed. "That means they're…" She paused to do the math.

"They cost me roughly fifteen grand a piece," Nathan said. "They're the same dimensions as the ones the Albuquerque refinery poured twenty-four years ago, so they should work."

Lydia pressed her hand to her mouth. "And you bought a dozen? They couldn't be real, could they?"

Nathan held up his left hand and pointed to the wide

gold wedding band on his ring finger. "They're as pure as this. The genuine article."

"My God," she murmured, looking at Derek. "You're not *that* persuasive."

"Don't let Nathan's biker look fool you," Derek said. "He's stinking rich. And he owed me a favor that I decided to collect."

"There's more to this," she said. "What's going on?"

It was Nathan who replied. "Last June, the Canyon Brotherhood were áccessories in the kidnapping of my son. Now after what they did in Amarillo, even if I didn't owe Derek a favor, I'd do whatever I could to help put them all behind bars."

"How's Jamie making out?" Derek asked.

Nathan smiled. It transformed his face, softening his chiseled features into startling handsomeness. "Great. He's growing like a weed. Kelly sends her regards. She would have come along, but she's feeling too queasy to travel these days."

"Is she sick?"

His smile grew into a satisfied grin. "Pregnant." He pushed back his sleeve to check his watch. "They're holding the plane for me. I've got to go."

Derek shook his hand. "Thanks for the help, chief."

"Sure. As long as you realize this makes us even."

Lydia watched him leave, then turned to Derek. "Who is he, anyway?"

Derek glanced at Sandra, who still appeared to be busy on the phone, then tipped his head toward the door. "Grab a jacket and we'll talk outside."

The sky was overcast when they stepped out of the house. The firs at the edge of the cliff swayed in the breeze as dark-bellied clouds were gathering on the western horizon. Although no one else was around, the traces of Sandra's people were everywhere. The normally empty clearing that stretched between the garage and the gates was crowded with the nondescript sedans favored by the FBI.

Derek bypassed the iron benches near the front door and started walking toward the firs beside the garage. He waited until they were well out of earshot from the house before he spoke. "Nathan owns the Pack Leader Express courier company."

"Why did you want to come outside to tell me that?" Lydia asked. "It's not a secret, is it?"

"No. Sandra knows who he is. She was there when he and Kelly got Jamie back. But she doesn't know anything about Payback."

Lydia pulled her jacket closed against the breeze as she walked beside him. The ground was uneven, so she had to concentrate on keeping her balance in her heels. "I take it Nathan is a member?"

"Yeah. Tony helped him found Pack Leader."

"That means Nathan was…"

"On the wrong side of the law," Derek said. "Now he's on the right side. He paid his debt to Tony in June by smashing a heroin smuggling ring."

They had reached the largest fir tree. She caught his arm to stop him. "Derek, I can't understand why the police don't know about Payback. From everything you've told me, it's truly an admirable network, even though Tony does seem harsh about penalizing people when they're late."

"Tony believes in justice, but he doesn't like the police."

"Why not? That doesn't make sense."

"This is why I wanted to talk to you in private. I can

see how hard all of this is on you. You're dredging up your worst nightmares and are willing to use them to catch McAllister, but I haven't forgotten that it was my promise to Tony that got you involved in this scheme." Derek covered her hand, holding it against his arm. "That's why you deserve to know the whole truth about Tony Monaco."

She tried to tug her hand free but he wrapped his fingers around hers to firm his grip. She glared. "This is too familiar, Derek. Just when I think you've told me everything, there's something else I don't know. How much more is there?"

"Do you want to hear this or not?"

"Why tell me at all?"

"Because once we leave here for the hotel, I probably won't have the chance to talk to you alone again, and I wanted to set the record straight."

"Fine. You want to clear your conscience."

"No, Lydia. I've been working at that for seven years." He released her hand. "A few words aren't going to make a difference now."

Her annoyance with him for withholding yet another piece of the truth dissolved as quickly as it had arisen. He'd said this was hard on her, but she knew that working with his former supervisor was hard on him, too. "All right," she said. "I'm listening."

"I'm not going to pretty it up. Tony Monaco is a legitimate businessman now, but he wasn't always. He used to be the heir to a criminal organization that the FBI tried to crack for four generations."

"Good Lord." She braced her hand against the trunk of the tree. "You make it sound as if he was some kind of mob boss."

"That's one way to put it. By the standards of the

criminal world, he wasn't just a boss, he was royalty. His organization brought in more money than the gross national product of a lot of countries."

It took a while for the full impact of the truth to settle, yet in a way, it wasn't that hard to grasp. Maybe it was because she'd had so many other shocks lately, she was becoming used to handling them. She thought of the priceless artwork that hung in Tony's house, the wealth that was evident at every turn. She hadn't considered the possibility that the wealth hadn't been acquired honestly. "Are you sure he went straight?"

"Positive," Derek said. "He changed his ways, but he couldn't change his reputation. That's why he moves around so much, and it's why he rigged this house like a fortress. He still has powerful enemies on both sides of the law."

The state-of-the-art security system took on new significance. So did a lot of other things. "That explains Sandra's tone when she spoke about him."

"Right."

"And it's why you sounded so alarmed when you found out I invited the FBI to his house."

He lifted his shoulders in a stiff shrug. "I'm not sure if Tony would appreciate the irony. I doubt if Sandra does, either. She was one of the cops who tried to nail him and couldn't."

"This is incredible," she murmured. "It was fantastic enough when I thought Tony was just a wealthy eccentric, but for a former gangster to devote himself to a project like Payback…" She shook her head. "How could he go from mob boss to justice crusader?"

He hesitated, then took her hand and turned toward the garage. "Come with me. I want to show you something."

Instead of opening the big overhead door, he took her through the small side entrance and flipped on the lights. The interior was deep enough to hold two rows of vehicles, but aside from Derek's Jeep, the rest were covered with tarps. Derek led the way toward the back wall. "These all belong to Tony," he said. "I keep the tags current for him so he can use them when he visits."

Lydia couldn't tell much about the covered shapes except that they were low-slung, so they were probably sports cars. "There must be a fortune in here."

"Yeah, but this one is the most interesting." He stopped beside the last car in the back row and lifted the tarp.

The object that sat in the corner appeared to be nothing but a twisted mass of metal. The only hints that it had once been a car were the curve of a wheel and the glint of chrome. Lydia stared. "Oh, my God. Why would anyone want to keep this?"

"Tony never talks about it, but I believe it's got something to do with why he went straight." He moved his hand along a piece of crumpled metal that bore a small, shield-shaped hood ornament. "It used to be a Porsche. This particular model was sold ten years ago, the same year that Tony grew a conscience."

She stared at the wreck. "How could anyone survive that?"

"The real question is, what would they do if they did?"

She thought about that for a while, then moved her gaze to Derek. "Oh, you are good."

He tipped an imaginary hat. "Why, thank you, ma'am."

She laughed. The sound startled her, echoing from

the cavernous building in a way that amplified itself before it returned. For a second she felt as if she had gone back to those first, magical days with Derek, before she'd learned the truth, when she'd eagerly soaked in every scrap of his attention. When she'd first started falling in love. She pressed her hand over her chest. Love? There was that word again.

"It isn't like bells," he said.

"Bells?"

"Your laugh. It's like the sound of that stream in the clearing where we spent our first night together." He smiled. "As if the water's rushing over the rocks so fast it's laughing about it."

It had been too long since she'd seen him smile. When he did, he put his whole face into it, from the creases in his cheeks to the laugh lines around his beautiful eyes. She loved his smile. She backed up until she bumped into the car behind her, then leaned her hips against the tarp-covered fender.

His smile faded. "You don't have to wear those shoes if they give you trouble. Your sweats and sneakers would work just as well for the cameras."

"I'm not that fragile."

"I realize you're an extraordinarily strong woman, Lydia. I admire your courage. I'm just worried that Sandra's going too far with the wardrobe."

"Thanks for your concern, Derek," she said. "And thank you for telling me about Tony. I'm glad you were willing to trust me."

He replaced the cover on the wrecked Porsche. "Let's just say you're not the only one who wants to change their pattern."

"I'm sorry for sniping at you yesterday with Sandra. I was..." Frustrated. Confused. "I wasn't in the best mood."

"Hey, you're entitled to take all the shots you want. We're a long way from even."

"No, Derek. These past few days have made me realize something. You were right. If you had told me the truth at the outset, I would have refused to look for the gold. I didn't have the self-confidence to face my memories. Your interest in me helped me with that."

"My *interest* wasn't noble, Lydia." He moved in front of her. "It was selfish."

She braced her hands on the car hood and tilted her head to look up at him. Even here in a dim garage amid shrouded cars, the most unromantic location imaginable, he could make her heart pound. "It was mutual."

He stepped closer, his toes nudging hers. "That's another reason I brought you outside. I want to talk about what happens next."

"What do you mean?"

"Whether or not McAllister and the Brotherhood swallow the bait and take the gold, after the press conference, your part in this will be over."

"But the gold is still out there."

"That doesn't matter. You're going to go public and say that you found it, and the authorities are going to back up your claim. As far as the rest of the world is concerned, the search is over."

"My God. I hadn't thought of that. If everyone believes the bullion has been found…"

"The legend of Zack's lost gold will be put to rest. The treasure hunters and the media should leave you alone."

"And I won't need to find the gold," she said slowly.

"That's right."

"It will be out of my life. I'll be free of it."

He stroked her cheek, then wound one of her freshly

reddened curls around his finger. "In theory, the Brotherhood will have no reason to come after you, but to be on the safe side, it would be better if you don't go home until they're caught."

In truth, she hadn't thought of going home since she'd left Denver, because she had nothing there she wanted to go back to. What she really wanted was to stay here with Derek and explore these feelings that were growing inside her. Was it love? And this time, was it real? "What are you suggesting?"

"I've already spoken with Sandra about this. Until McAllister is behind bars, she's willing to have the FBI provide you with protection."

Lydia tried not to feel disappointed. After all, she'd been the one who had insisted their relationship was temporary. Loudly and often. Most recently yesterday, just before they'd nearly made love on the stairs. "Don't you want me to stay with you?"

He gave her a look that was hot enough to knock the breath from her lungs, then placed his palms on the fender on either side of her hips and leaned over her so that his chest brushed her breasts. "If this was only about what I want, we wouldn't be having this conversation in a garage, we'd be having it in a bed."

It didn't take much. Only a touch, a look, and her body ached for his. She arched her back, easing herself more firmly against him.

He turned his face toward her neck and inhaled hard. "Do you have any idea how hard it is for me to keep my hands off you?"

She tipped her head back, drawing in his scent and warmth. "I, uh, noticed you liked my new outfit."

"Sure. What man wouldn't? But it's not what you wear or what you do to the outside. It's who you are on the inside." He touched his forehead to hers. "And I can't forget I was your first."

My first and only, she thought, closing her eyes. She would never forget that, either. She could feel the restraint that hummed through his frame. It was sexier than if he'd caressed her.

"But this isn't about what I want, Lydia," he said. "Your safety is my priority."

"I'd be safe with you."

He rolled his forehead along hers in a slow negative. "If McAllister and the Brotherhood aren't stopped within two weeks, I won't have this house, and I can't take you on the run with me. That's why it would be better if we make arrangements for your protection now."

She brought her hands between them and pushed at his chest. "On the run? What are you talking about?"

He lifted his head. His gaze swirled with desire, and with a shadow of regret.

"Oh, God," she murmured. "There's something else you haven't told me, isn't there?"

"Lydia, if I don't keep my word to Tony, I'll lose more than my house. He's going to take back everything his help gave me."

"What do you mean by everything? Your business?"

"My business, my Jeep, my equipment, anything I acquired since we made our bargain. It's what I agreed to when I joined Payback. If I fail to pay Tony back, I leave the Payback network exactly as I came in."

"You said you'd be on the run. From Tony?"

"No. From the loan shark who sold him my markers."

"What?"

He grasped her wrists and straightened up, tugging her off the car to stand in front of him. "That was part of the deal. If I don't keep my word, Tony's going to sell those markers back."

"Derek, no! He wouldn't. That's criminal!"

"Tony might have gone legit, but he didn't come that far from his roots. He's not running a charity."

"But that loan shark had threatened to—"

"I'll deal with it, Lydia. I just can't take you with me while I do. It wouldn't be safe."

She locked her hands behind his waist and pressed closer, shuddering as she felt the bulge against her stomach. The idea of Derek being hurt was unthinkable. "Sandra can help. Get her to arrest the loan shark."

"I'll deal with it," he repeated. "And if the sting works, I won't have to. The important thing is that you'll be taken care of either way."

"I don't want to be taken care of. I've had enough of that. It's high time someone worried about you."

"Hey, I'll be fine."

"Will you? You've been on your own practically all your life and you've gotten too accustomed to keeping it that way. I care what happens to you. Derek, I—" The word was there, trying to get out...until she felt the tension in his body.

His muscles were stiff, as if he were preparing himself for a blow even worse than the prospect of being hunted down by a vengeful loan shark.

Did he realize what she was about to say? He'd been so astute when it came to reading her feelings, had he guessed that she'd fallen in love with him?

And that's when the final truth hit her. Derek *wanted* to be alone. She was in love with a man who didn't want to love anyone.

She leaned back to meet his gaze. "What happens if

the sting works, Derek? What then? Would you want me to stay?"

"You wouldn't need protection. You'd be free to do whatever you want."

"That's not what I asked."

He didn't blink or recoil, his expression didn't change, yet everything about him seemed to withdraw a notch. "You know how I live, Lydia. I'm gone more than I'm here. And you know why I need my job."

She did know. She understood why he was this way. It had started when he'd been eleven years old, hiding in a casino while he waited for his mother to come back. He'd been too proud to ask for help, too hurt to admit he cared. So he'd learned to use risk to fill the void where love should have been.

He'd been honest about this from the very beginning. He traveled the world feeding his need for adventure, so he made sure any relationship would be only temporary. He'd never led her on. He hadn't promised her anything more than enjoyment. A good flight. In his own way, he'd been honorable.

But damn, he was a frustrating man to love. "All this time, I'd thought that I was the timid one."

"Lydia…"

"You shoot rapids and climb mountains to get your adrenaline rush. You're just fine about using sex to get your blood pumping. You can analyze and manipulate other people's emotions, but do you know something, Derek?" She tapped her fingertips against his chest. "You're scared stiff of opening your heart."

During the past month, the press had been Lydia's enemy. They had hounded her at every step, turning her life into a fishbowl. The sight of vans with satellite dishes and reporters with microphones had sent her scurrying for the privacy of her basement. They still made her stomach knot, yet this time, she wasn't running. Like the other nightmares she had faced lately, this one had lost its power.

Squaring her glasses on her nose, she looked around the room. Lights from television cameras glared whitely, all but washing out the glitter from the chandeliers overhead. This hotel banquet hall was normally used for functions such as wedding receptions or fundraising dinners, but tonight it was packed with representatives from the major networks and newspapers.

The site of the press conference was a trade-off between security and accessibility. Lydia could see the familiar faces of FBI agents at each entrance, and she knew more were stationed around the hotel, but they were keeping a low profile. She knew she would be safe, yet for the sting to work, the gold had to appear to be vulnerable.

"Miss Smith, how did you find it?"

She looked at the reporter who had spoken. So far, the press were staying behind the rope barrier the hotel had provided. "It wasn't difficult. As you all know, I was an eyewitness to the robbery."

"Where was it?"

"Exactly where I saw my father leave it."

"Care to be more specific?"

"No. Next question."

Another reporter pushed toward the front of the room. "It's been a week since you staged your disappearance. Why did you wait so long to go public?"

She stood a little straighter, enjoying the extra few inches her heels added to her height. "I had some personal matters to attend to."

"What was your first stop? A beauty parlor?"

There was a scattering of laughter at the question. Lydia hadn't missed the stares and double takes when she'd first made her entrance. She knew she looked transformed—that had been the point of the dress, the hair dye and the makeup Sandra had helped her apply.

Yet as Derek had once told her, the transformation hadn't only been on the surface. She wasn't a different woman, she was the woman she was meant to be. "Absolutely," she replied. "It was long overdue."

More questions followed, similar to the ones that had been shouted at her last month whenever she had ventured into public. Lydia handled them carefully, mindful of the briefing Sandra had given her. She made sure to allude to the original robbery as often as she could, and had nothing but praise for her father.

"Zachary Dorland may have made a mistake when he stole that shipment of bullion," she said. "Yet that didn't change who he was. He was a good father and a good man. I loved him very much." She cleared her throat. "This is why, in honor of his memory, I'm restoring the gold to the United States government."

"Where's the gold now?"

This was the question she'd been waiting for. She turned to glance at the long, shiny steel trunk that sat on the floor at the base of the wall behind her. It was flanked by two men who wore security guard uniforms, but like the press conference itself, they weren't what they seemed. One was an FBI agent and the other was Derek.

He looked completely different from the easygoing cowboy she was used to seeing. Like the agent beside him, he bore the closed expression of what she'd heard referred to as a game face. With his hat pulled low over his forehead and mirrored sunglasses concealing his eyes, he gave no indication that he was watching her, but she had felt his gaze from the moment she'd stepped to the cluster of microphones.

She wished she could take back what she'd said to him in the garage. Then again, she wished she hadn't had to say it. Love wasn't supposed to be that complicated, was it?

"Considering the amount involved," she said, recalling her briefing, "the bulk of the bullion is being held in safekeeping at a local bank until transportation can be arranged." She gestured to the trunk. "But I've brought a small portion with me if you care to take pictures."

A restless hum spread through the room as she walked to the trunk. From the corner of her eye, she saw the rope barrier sway as several people crowded closer. They were stopped when a second pair of security guards positioned themselves in the way. Derek gave her an almost imperceptible nod. Without further delay, she opened the lid to reveal the neatly stacked gold bars.

The hum rose to an excited babble. Cameras flashed, sending glints dancing across the bullion. Lydia's vision blurred with an afterimage, as if the gold had been lit by sunlight instead of camera flashes….

"Miss Smith!" someone shouted. "Can we get a shot of you holding a bar?"

She bit her lip. The unfamiliar taste of lipstick under her teeth helped her to regain her focus. She reached into the trunk and closed her hand around the nearest bar. This was the important part. She'd dangled the bait, now she had to invite the Brotherhood to take it.

As soon as she felt the smooth metal beneath her fingers, an image burst through her mind. She saw the tumbled heap of gold, but it was no longer bright, it was gleaming like silver in the moonlight....

Not now! she thought.

"Miss Smith, this way!"

The bar was heavier than it looked. Her hand didn't feel large enough to hold it. She inhaled to gather her strength, but her lungs filled with the scent of diesel fuel and the stale, coppery tang of blood.

A firm hand gripped her elbow. She looked up and saw that Derek had moved to her side.

"They're worried she'll take off with it," someone called. "Just like her old man."

There was a ripple of laughter. Lydia clenched her jaw and turned around, her knuckles whitening on the gold bar. She held the bar against her midriff to ensure her dress was in the picture. The flash of cameras was practically blinding. "This doesn't belong to me," she said. "By this time tomorrow, it will be restored to its rightful owner."

"Message delivered," Derek murmured from behind her. "You can wrap this up."

She gave a farewell wave, then turned quickly and dropped the bar into the trunk, anxious to get rid of it. The feel of it on her skin was making her gag. The bar hit the others with a dull clank, echoing through her memory, tangling with the raw, wrenching sound of sobs.

Her vision blurred again, this time with tears. There was so much sadness yet to remember.

"Deep breaths, Lydia," Derek said. "You did great."

Hazily, she saw four FBI agents move in to pick up the trunk. They would be taking it to the armored truck, a highly visible target, that was waiting outside the back door. This was what they'd planned. She had all but rolled out a red carpet to anyone interested in stealing this bullion. Now it was only a question of whether the Brotherhood would be willing to settle for it.

"Congratulations, Lydia," Sandra said, stepping forward. "You did an excellent job."

"Thank you."

"I'll escort you upstairs. You must be anxious to get out of those heels."

She nodded. The FBI had taken over the second floor of the hotel when they had vacated Tony's house. Sandra's suite would serve as their command post for the duration of the operation. It would also be Lydia's home until she could return to her own.

"We'll give the convoy with the gold a chance to clear out first," Derek said. "If the Brotherhood are here, that will draw them away."

Sandra glanced at the departing press corps, then pulled her phone from her purse and headed for another agent.

Lydia looked at Derek, and the sadness from the past spilled into the present. Love tangled with loss and fear and the slick feel of gold on her palm. Maybe he had the right idea. It would be easier to hide from love than to let in the pain....

"Are you all right?" Derek asked. "You looked wobbly there for a second."

"I can't stop the memories," she murmured. "There are too many parallels. Everything I do seems to trigger more."

A commotion arose at the far end of the room. A crisp, crackling sound swelled through the air. "Fire!" someone cried.

Lydia spun to look. Flames licked along the wallpaper toward the ceiling, sending smoke billowing through the chandeliers. Derek clamped his arm around her back and steered her toward the nearest emergency exit just as the rhythmic buzz of a fire alarm cut through the crowd.

Seconds before they reached the side door, a news crew that must have already gone outside was pushing their way back in. A short man with a television camera propped on his shoulder stumbled into Derek, then pivoted suddenly, swinging the heavy camera into Derek's face.

It happened so fast, Lydia had barely realized he'd been struck before Derek spun her behind him and delivered two swift blows to his attacker.

The camera crashed to the floor as the man staggered backward. At the same instant, his companion drew a Taser from beneath his jacket and thrust it at Derek.

He jerked, momentarily stunned by the charge that shot through his body. That was all the advantage the men needed. Within seconds, they had him on the floor, their boots thudding into his back and his head.

Lydia felt the blows as if they were landing on her. She lunged for his attackers. "Stop!"

Someone grabbed her arms from behind and dragged her away from him. "You're coming with us, bitch."

She knew that voice. She recognized the cigarette and motor oil smell that clung to his clothes. It was Ralph, the man who had sliced off her hair.

Disbelief warred with panic. This wasn't supposed to happen. There were agents posted at every entrance. How could anyone have gotten past them?

She screamed for help, but her cry was lost in the mayhem that was unfolding as the crowd streamed for every exit. The fire must have been set as a diversion, she realized. Smoke stung her eyes, mixing with her tears. She twisted to look back at Derek. He lay unmoving, blood masking his face. He was so pale, so still....

I love you, baby. Remember that. I don't want to leave you.

Grief swelled in her heart, but she couldn't tell whether it was from now or then. No. She couldn't lose him. "Derek!" she cried.

"Shut up," Ralph muttered. The tip of a knife pricked the skin beneath her ear, sending a trickle of warmth down her neck.

Fresh air rushed over her face as she was propelled outside. Earl and Pete fell in on either side of her as they moved through the parking lot. Sirens sounded in the distance. There were people everywhere, but they probably wouldn't be able to see her sandwiched between the men. They headed for a white van painted with the call letters of a local television station.

Lydia's terror deepened. Four bodies lay motionless on the pavement behind the van's back bumper. Another two were slumped against the doors of a dark sedan that was parked beside it.

Oh, God. Those were FBI agents.

She tipped her chin away from the knife blade. "Why are you doing this? I don't have the gold. It's in the armored truck. Taking me won't get it for you."

Ralph shoved her into the back of the van. "For your sake, you better hope you're wrong."

Chapter 12

The bogeyman was coming again. Lydia could tell it was him by the tap of his cane and the hitch in his step. She could feel the dread that froze her blood whenever he came near. His smell was old and sour, like starch mixed with vinegar. His face was a nightmare that wouldn't end.

The springs of the cot creaked as Lydia pushed herself to her feet. The concrete floor was cold. She'd lost her shoes in her struggles. Why did she always seem to lose her shoes? She turned to face the door, her heart pounding so hard her chest ached.

Stop it! she told herself. He wasn't the bogeyman. He wasn't the embodiment of her fears, he was just a man. An evil, sick criminal. She wouldn't allow him the power to terrify her.

But, oh God, it was hard to keep the whimper inside. She couldn't run because McAllister's men had handcuffed her to the metal frame of the cot. Not by her wrists—they were too small and had slipped through the handcuffs. They'd locked one cuff around her ankle instead.

How could she have chafed at her father's coddling? How could she have compared it to a prison? This was the real thing. The two days she'd spent in this tiny, windowless closet of a room already seemed like an eternity.

There was the scrape of a key and the door swung open. Hart McAllister, followed by the stocky man, Pete, moved into the room.

Lydia curled her nails into her palms and clenched her jaw. She would not let them see her fear. She refused to break down and blubber, in spite of the cramp that knifed through her right foot from the cold floor and the stinging in her ankle where the cuff had rubbed her skin raw.

McAllister stacked his hands on the curved handle of his cane and studied her. At first glance, he didn't look like a monster. He had the chiseled, distinguished appearance of an officer on an army recruiting poster. The illusion didn't extend to his gaze—it was as cold and hard as the floor. He nodded to Pete, who moved past her to pick up the plate that had held her breakfast.

Lydia had wanted to refuse their food out of principle, but she realized she had to eat something to keep up her strength. Derek would come for her soon.

But how? The last time she'd seen him, he'd been motionless and bleeding in a room filled with smoke. What if he hadn't made it out?

No. She couldn't give in to that fear, either. He was alive. She had to believe that, because she couldn't consider the alternative.

Pete turned with her plate, deliberately brushing the back of his hand across her breast as he walked by. She recoiled, but stopped herself from striking out at him. She'd been thoroughly and humiliatingly searched before she'd been brought here. If she'd worn a tracking device as she had initially intended, it would have been found.

Yet even if she'd been tracked, how could anyone rescue her? From what she'd seen before she'd been locked in this room, this place was guarded as closely as a military base.

McAllister shifted closer, his shoes gritting across the floor. "You look more like her every day."

She forced herself to meet his gaze. "Let me go," she said, just as she had each morning. "You want the gold, not me."

He gave no sign that he realized she was echoing her mother's words. "The bullion is rightfully mine. The Canyon Brotherhood will make good use of it."

"You forced my father to steal it by kidnapping my mother. It was never yours, any more than my mother was."

"They both were mine. It was your father who was the thief. He took Rose, then he took my gold." His fingers tightened on his cane. "It's time to settle the score."

"That's what this is about, isn't it?" she asked. "It isn't about what that gold could buy—you're settling the score, that's all. Do your men realize they're being used to carry out your personal agenda?"

He lifted one hand from his cane and backhanded her across the jaw.

She staggered, snapping the handcuff chain taut. Stars danced across her eyes. In a blink, the stars became moonlight on gold. White dots on a black dress.

Memories rose in a choking cloud as the present merged with the past.

Daddy was coming soon. That's what Mommy had promised, but she was cold now and wouldn't wake up no matter how hard Lydia shook her.

Lights glowed from the darkness, moving along the floor of the gully toward her. The noise of a big truck bounced from the rocks. Lydia scrambled to her feet. "Daddy?"

But it wasn't her father. It was the bogeyman. He'd come back with another truck. He'd wrecked the first one because he couldn't work the pedals right. He didn't walk right, either. His foot dragged on the ground, stirring up dust that looked like smoke in the headlights.

Lydia grabbed her mother's arm and tried to pull her backward, wanting to hide both of them.

Yet the man only walked as far as the heap of gold, picked up an armful of bars and carried them back to his truck....

"Sergeant Wilcox," McAllister snapped. "Give her the statement."

Lydia touched her jaw, using the pain to help her focus. The memories had been surfacing more and more frequently. Each time they did, another few pieces fell into place. She wondered if she'd live long enough to remember it all.

"Yes, sir." Pete withdrew a folded piece of paper from a pocket in his fatigues. He snapped it open and held it out to Lydia. "When the Colonel tells you, read this aloud."

She skimmed the handwritten lines. Her pulse, already elevated, thudded so hard she felt faint. "They're not going to agree to this."

"I think they will. It worked before." McAllister took a cell phone from his uniform and dialed a number. "Here is the proof you asked for," he said into the phone. "Listen carefully if you want her to live." He pressed the phone to her ear. "Read it," he ordered.

"Miss Smith? Are you all right?"

At the sound of Sandra's voice, a lump came to Lydia's throat. "Yes. I'm fine. How's Derek? Is he okay? Did—"

McAllister snatched the phone away and rapped his cane against her shin. "Read it."

Lydia took a deep breath and started to read. "The price for my life is the gold my father stole..."

Derek fisted his hands, his body tensing in helpless frustration as he listened to the tape once more. Lydia's voice was steady. She sounded scared but healthy. She had asked about him.

Damn, he never should have encouraged her to go public. He shouldn't have trusted the feds to protect her, either. To them, she was just a tool to be used, a means to an end. What happened to her was secondary. Their priority was stopping the Brotherhood.

Sounded familiar, didn't it?

Cursing, he raked his fingers through his hair. At the sudden movement, pain knifed through his side from his cracked ribs. He forced himself to breathe shallowly through his nose until it passed. "I should have seen it," he said. "It's not about the gold, it's about winning. McAllister's trying to rewrite history. He's determined to get the bullion the same way he did before, only this time he's using Lydia instead of her mother."

Sandra handed the tape recorder to the nearest agent, then pushed aside the edge of the drapes and looked down at the hotel parking lot. Since Lydia's abduction, the FBI operation had grown to include personnel from practically every other law enforcement agency in the country. Sandra's suite was still the headquarters for her team—few people looked as if they had slept. "I'm no longer in charge, Derek," she said. "The Canyon Brotherhood have been deemed a terrorist organization. Homeland Security is calling the shots—I'm just the telephone contact."

Derek followed her gaze. Among the sedans and cargo vans that crowded the parking lot, a bulky RV bristled with antennae and satellite dishes. It didn't belong to a television station. The lid had been clamped down hard on the media—there wasn't a camera or reporter allowed within three hundred yards. The RV was the joint task force's mobile communications center. "What's their plan?" he asked.

"You're a civilian. I shouldn't be telling you anything." The fax machine on the desk clicked on. She turned to watch the progress of the page. "You're also a mess. They should have kept you in the hospital."

He touched the gauze that covered the stitches in his forehead. His right eye was blackened, but the swelling had gone down enough so that it no longer impaired his vision. "I've had worse. They're planning to stall, aren't they?"

Sandra's mouth thinned.

"They're going to bluff while they use the dialogue over the ransom to get a fix on McAllister's location," he continued. "He's so obsessed with getting that gold, he's bound to get sloppy."

"The big boys have access to technology that I don't," she said. "All they needed was for him to stick his head up once—"

"Needed?" Derek repeated. "Damn it, they *already* know."

"I didn't say that."

He glanced around the suite. Everyone was busy working the phones or computers. He and Sandra had the privacy that only a crowd could offer. "Tell me they're going to secure Lydia's safety before they move in."

"I'm not authorized to tell you anything."

He lowered his voice. "Don't sideline me now. I need to be part of this."

"Even if you were still on my team, I'd have reservations. You're too close to this. Anyone can see you're emotionally involved."

"You're right about that. I've got emotions involved that I didn't know I had, and the hell of it is, I'm not sorry."

"You've changed."

"I hope I have. I used to be proud of how well I could detach myself from my work, but what I thought was my greatest strength turned out to be my greatest weakness. Maybe if I hadn't been so busy trying to be detached, I wouldn't have trashed my life seven years ago."

"I never wanted to fire you, Derek, but you left me no alternative."

"I know. I never blamed you. I might have been good at my job, but I wasn't much of a man."

"You had an addiction."

"It was only a symptom. I'm still working on solving the problem."

She studied him in silence, her gaze probing his.

He returned her gaze unflinchingly. He'd punished himself for his mistakes long enough. There was no point dwelling on his honor or lack of it. What would the life he'd built matter if he lost Lydia?

At the thought, pain shot through his chest. It wasn't from his injured ribs, it was from a source much deeper, a place he'd guarded for decades. And opening it up hurt.

This was a hell of a time to realize that Lydia had been right. He was scared. Terrified. He hadn't wanted to admit what he felt for her. That would have been too big of a gamble. He'd even tried to push her away.

But he'd been deluding himself. She was already a part of him.

He could only pray he hadn't realized it too late.

"Sandra," he said. "McAllister is trying to rewrite history, but I've got some history of my own I need to fix. I can't do it alone. Please, give me the chance to put this right."

Her jaw flexed, as if she were chewing the inside of her lip. Finally, she checked her watch and nodded crisply. "The strike force that's planning the raid is assembling in the conference room in ten minutes," she said. "And by the way—" she gave him a tight smile "—welcome back."

Derek studied the satellite images that had been projected on the screen. From above, the Canyon Brotherhood's new compound seemed impregnable. The abandoned copper mine they had taken over was nestled into the side of a mountain. Apart from the area that had been blasted flat to accommodate the ore processing buildings and the mine offices, nothing but sheer rock walls surrounded it. Only one narrow road, full of switchbacks, carved its way up the slope.

The location was less than two hundred miles from

Denver, near the Wyoming border. Derek had figured they had to be close, since McAllister had seen the Denver newspaper with Lydia and her father's pictures.

He leaned one shoulder against the wall as he glanced at the men and women who were gathered around the room. Along with Sandra and a few of her colleagues, there were representatives from the ATF, the state police and the treasury department, all top-notch people. The group even included some commandos from a crack Special Forces squadron out of Fort Bragg. Officially, the soldiers were here only as advisors, like Derek. From the grim looks on their faces, though, he doubted whether they were going to let jurisdictional technicalities hold them back from participating any more than he would.

The satellite image of the compound wavered, then switched to a pattern of colored blotches. One of the soldiers, a trim, blond woman in the uniform of an army captain, pointed to the screen. "This infrared scan shows there are manned defensive positions at each bend of the switchback as well as around the plateau."

"The army trained those guys well," one of the ATF agents muttered. "They know what they're doing." He patted his shirt pocket as if looking for a cigarette pack, then took out a stick of gum. "They've got an unobstructed line of sight for almost a full 360 degrees."

"Which would make an aerial assault problematic."

"We want to avoid a firefight at all costs if we're going to recover the Brotherhood's records," he said, popping the gum in his mouth. "Otherwise, we won't be sure we've rounded up the entire group."

"A firefight would endanger the hostage," Sandra said. "We need to catch them by surprise."

"They appear to be using the oblong building in the

center of the plateau as their living quarters." The captain used a wand to indicate some of the orange blotches. "That's the only one that is showing body heat patterns. The hostage and the records are likely being kept there."

"Stealth is our only option." A large man in fatigues spoke up from where he stood near the back wall. His blond hair was cropped military short, and a network of deep scars crisscrossed one side of his face. "Captain, do you have any information on the mine itself?"

"Yes, Sergeant." A line drawing came up on the screen. "This is a cross-section of the mountain, showing the location of the tunnels. As you can see, the main shaft begins at the plateau and has no other exits."

Derek straightened up and walked to the screen. "What's this?" he asked, pointing to a thin line that slanted upward from the main tunnel.

"According to the plans, it's an air shaft."

"Is it guarded?"

The captain switched back to the infrared image, then to the original satellite shot. "Apparently not. The slope where it exits is only a few degrees off vertical. They must have considered it inaccessible."

"Not for me. If I get a rope up there, can the rest of you follow?"

The ATF agent who had spoken earlier frowned at him. "That's a big 'if.'"

"Compared to the climbs I've done," Derek said, "that's a walk in the park."

One of the other men in fatigues whistled softly. "Friend, you look as if you already fell down one mountain. You sure you're up for this?"

Derek crossed his arms. The grinding of his ribs was only a distant discomfort. He hadn't needed painkillers—the adrenaline that was coursing through his body was more potent than any drug. "I've never been more sure of anything in my life," he said. "Whatever the odds, this is one risk I'm going to take."

"Sounds personal."

"As personal as it gets. You got a problem with that?"

"Nope," the commando said. "It got personal for us the minute those Brotherhood cowards put on uniforms, called themselves patriots and murdered thirty-one real heroes." He glanced at his scarred companion. "So it looks like we follow our friend here in the back door and crash the party. What do you think, Rafe?"

"I'm good to go, Flynn. Major?"

The officer who had been standing quietly to one side throughout the meeting dipped his chin once and moved his gaze around the room. "Let's rock and roll, people. It's time for some payback."

Lydia knelt on the ground and locked her arms around her mother. They were almost to the rocks but she couldn't pull her any farther. The pile of gold was nearly gone. The man was moving more slowly now, his leg dragging behind him worse every time he carried bars to his truck. Through the fog of dust, she could see the groove his shoe had left in the dirt.

The bars clinked as he dropped another armload on top of the rest. Lydia was trying to be quiet but the sound of the gold made her whimper. She hated it. She hated the gold and that man. "Mommy, please," she whispered. "Wake up, wake up, wake up."

But her mother was as cold and still as the night.

Lydia tightened her arms and rocked her mother back and forth the way Mommy did when she had a bad dream. She knew something bad was going to happen when that pile of gold was gone.

Suddenly, the night was no longer still. Lydia could hear a rumbling noise. Lights blinked in the darkness.

The bogeyman snatched more bars and moved back to his truck. He tried to speed up, but he dropped a bar in the dirt. The lights came closer, lining his face in white as he stooped to pick up the gold.

"You son of a bitch!" It was Daddy's voice, but not his voice. It was loud and scary. "Where are they?"

The bogeyman was no longer alone. Another man moved into the foggy light from the headlights. Lydia saw raven-black hair and a blue checkered shirt like her father's. She clasped her mother's hand and rose to her knees. "Daddy!" she screamed.

His head snapped toward her.

The bogeyman twisted, ramming his shoulder into Lydia's father's stomach, knocking him to the ground.

"Daddy!"

Her father rolled to his feet and swung at the bogeyman. There were more noises, solid, hard punches and bad words. Lydia squeezed her eyes shut and rocked faster. She didn't want to see. Please, she wanted to wake up.

"Lydia? Where are you, baby?"

It was Daddy's voice, but it was still wrong. It hurt like the sand that had scraped her knees.

"Rose? Darling, answer me."

Lydia realized the punches had stopped. Her father was the only one she could hear. She opened her eyes and there he was, just as Mommy had promised. He had found them.

But he didn't make everything all right. He fell to his knees beside her and folded in half, his head dropping against her mother's chest. He made sounds as if he was crying, deep, tearing sobs that echoed from the rocks, but he couldn't be crying because Daddy never cried.

She let go of her mother's hand and crawled to his side. "Daddy, I want to go home."

He scooped her into his arms. He was shaking, and he was holding her so tight she started to cry, too. "We can't, sweet pea. It's too late."

Lydia jerked awake, her heard pounding. The dream was over, but the nightmare wasn't.

She rolled to her back. Pain ringed her ankle where the handcuff pulled tight. The metal chain rattled against the cot. Shivering, she pulled the blanket to her chin. It was scratchy wool, and it smelled like mold. God, she wanted this to end.

A tear trickled from the corner of her eye and into her hair. She shouldn't be so eager for the end. It was going to come as soon as McAllister realized he would never get the ransom he'd demanded.

She knew now why her father had hidden the gold. He hadn't wanted McAllister to take it. Zachary had never planned to go back for it—he hadn't wanted *anyone* to have it. She could still feel his heartbreak as he'd mourned for her mother.

As if she'd summoned him from her nightmare, she heard the sliding steps of the bogeyman outside the door.

She wiped her eyes and sat up, flinging the blanket aside just as the key scraped in the lock. There were no windows in the room, but she could tell it was still night by the absence of the strip of daylight that showed under the door. Something was wrong.

Wrong? She choked down a bubble of hysteria. She was shackled and helpless, the prisoner of the madman who had destroyed her family. How much worse could it get?

The light in the ceiling switched on, spreading its stark glare down the concrete block walls and the dusty floor. The door swung open. Lydia slid the handcuff chain to the edge of the cot frame so she could get to her feet.

McAllister strode across the threshold, followed by Ralph. "Release her," he ordered.

Ralph glanced over his shoulder at the corridor as he dug in his pocket. "Sir, if we leave now—"

"Do as you're told, soldier." He rapped his cane across Ralph's wrist.

Ralph dropped to one knee to unlock her shackles. The steel fell away from Lydia's foot and clanked to the floor. Other noises came through the open door, rapid tapping sounds, like distant firecrackers or...

It was gunfire, Lydia realized. She leapt forward, trying to reach the door, but Ralph grabbed her ankle before she could go past, his fingers digging cruelly into the circle of raw skin. She cried out and kicked at him. He dodged her foot and flipped her onto the cot.

She bounced on the mattress and landed against the wall hard enough to knock the wind out of her. She gasped, trying to pull air into her lungs.

"Back to your post, Private," McAllister said. As Ralph departed, McAllister shifted his cane to his left hand. With his right, he pointed a revolver at Lydia. "You're coming with me."

Lydia looked from the gun to McAllister's face. The knife-sharp features were drawn tight and his eyes were glazed, as if he were in pain. "Who's out there?" she asked. "What's happening?"

He waved the gun barrel toward the door. "That's not your concern. Let's go."

She got back to her feet. She could hear shouts now. The gunfire came only in quick bursts, drawing rapidly closer. "No. I'm not going anywhere with you."

"You're mine, Rose."

Horror shuddered from her memory. "I'm not Rose."

He continued as if he hadn't heard her. "You're not getting away this time. My plan will work. You'll see."

"Lydia?"

It was Derek's voice, coming from the corridor, sounding strong and blessedly real. Thank God. He was alive, and he had found her. "Derek!" she cried. "I'm in here!"

As fast as a snake, McAllister aimed his gun toward the doorway just as a tall, black-clad figure moved into view. The man's face was covered by a black ski mask, but Lydia recognized him instinctively.

The horror deepened. This monster had taken away everyone else she had loved. He was going to take another.

It's too late.

"No!" Lydia screamed. She sprang at McAllister. "No more!"

The gun discharged as Lydia slammed into him from behind. The bullet struck the wall, sending chunks of cement across the room.

McAllister pivoted toward her, his face contorted into a grimace of rage. He jammed the gun against her neck. "You're mine, Rose!"

Once again, Lydia heard her mother's screams. Terror knew no boundaries of time as the past shoved its way into the present.

"Put the gun down, McAllister," Derek ordered. He pulled off his ski mask with one hand while he leveled a pistol with the other. "Your war is finished."

"Stay back or I shoot," he snarled.

Two more black-clad men stood in the doorway, their weapons pointed at McAllister. They had the bearing of soldiers, real ones, not the bitter impostors of the Brotherhood. "There's no escape, Colonel," one of them said. "Put down your gun. Your men have surrendered."

Lydia realized that the gunfire outside had ceased. The fight had ended as quickly as it had arisen.

"I'm giving the orders. Step aside." McAllister shoved the gun beneath Lydia's chin. "I want guaranteed safe passage or I kill her."

White dots danced behind Lydia's eyes. Gold sparkled in the sunlight. She heard her mother's voice, urging her to run.

But she wasn't going to hide or run. Never again. Not from anything. The past ended now.

With a strength that had been building for twenty-four years, Lydia whirled away from the gun, snatched McAllister's cane and swung it at his head.

The gun thudded to the floor. He screamed, staggered off balance and grasped her skirt. Fabric ripped. "Damn you, Rose!"

Lydia felt as if someone else's hands were gripping her own, guiding her actions. She swung the cane and hit McAllister again, splitting the skin over his cheekbone and sending him to his knees. The next blow caught him in the shoulder and knocked him to his side. He whimpered, trying to drag himself backward across the floor. She was winding up for a fourth one when Derek took her in his arms.

He was shaking, and he was holding her so tight, she could barely breathe.

The other men moved in to drag away McAllister.

Voices drifted in from the corridor, along with the crackle of radios and the sound of approaching helicopters.

"It's all over, Lydia," Derek said. "I've got you now."

She opened her fingers, and the cane clattered to the cement. The past stirred, shifted and settled. The pain and fear crumbled to dust. Only the love endured....

I love you, baby. Remember that. I never did leave you.

Chapter 13

Lydia held the blanket around her as the army helicopter lifted off from the clifftop. It banked over Tony's house and then headed east, its squat, dark silhouette disappearing into the glare of the rising sun. Like Derek, the commandos who had participated in the raid on the Canyon Brotherhood's stronghold hadn't needed to stay for the mopping up because officially, they hadn't been there.

The raid had been a resounding success, in large part because the members of the Brotherhood had been taken completely by surprise. The militia group was smashed, the Colonel and his men were in custody. Sandra and her FBI team, as well as a crowd of other law enforcement officials, would be busy processing the prisoners and the evidence at the old mine site for days.

No one had objected when Derek had announced he was taking Lydia home, least of all Lydia. She was physically exhausted and emotionally spent. The parallels between the present and the past were eerily close—McAllister and the gold had weaved their way through two generations. Her mind was still reeling from her recollections, and there was much she had yet to sort through.

But her feelings for Derek had never been clearer. Her heart swelled with love as she watched him approach. The skin around his eyes was mottled with bruises, a thick, white bandage covered his forehead, yet he still looked wonderful to her. "It was nice of your friends to drop us off," she said.

"They're a decent bunch. How's the ankle?"

"It's fine. The medic put something on that numbed it." She lifted one hand from the blanket to touch his face. "These must hurt."

He grasped her hand and kissed her fingertips. "They're not that bad. Your feet must be cold."

She flexed her toes against the ground. "I'm getting used to it."

He leaned over and scooped her into his arms. "I'll take you inside."

Lydia slipped her arms around his neck. Derek had been carrying her everywhere for the past few hours, supposedly because she'd lost her shoes, but she knew it was because he likely needed this contact as much as she did. "Could we stay out here for a while?" she asked. "I'd like to watch the sunrise."

"Whatever you want, Lydia." He carried her to one of the wrought iron benches in front of the house, then turned and sat with her on his lap. He tucked the blanket around her feet. "Jack gave me some pills that would help you sleep, if you'd like."

"Jack?"

"The medic." He stroked her hair. "I told Sandra you wouldn't be able to answer any questions until tomorrow. She's got enough to keep her busy until then."

"Yes, I bet she does. But I don't need pills, Derek. I don't want to sleep, and I don't need you to take care of me. I don't want to talk about Sandra or the Brotherhood or the gold. I want to talk about what happens next."

He cupped her head. "That's easy."

"Oh?"

"I'm going to kiss you."

"Derek—"

His lips trembled as they touched hers. The tenderness took her by surprise. From the moment he'd burst into her cell with those two commandos, he'd looked hard and determined, as boldly masculine as a man could get. She would have expected passion.

Yet this gentle whisper of his mouth on hers felt more intimate than any other kiss they'd shared. It was perfect, as fresh and full of promise as the dawn.

Smiling, she rested her head on his shoulder. "That was nice."

He took her hand and pressed a kiss to her knuckles. "I'm not finished."

Oh, he was more right than he knew. She wasn't going to let him push her away again. That was one positive thing that had come from her ordeal. By settling the past, she had truly broken free of her pattern. She'd accused Derek of being afraid to open his heart, but she'd been afraid, too. That was over. She loved him, and love wasn't something to hide from, it was worth fighting for. *This* was what her mother had been trying to tell her.

"But before we go on," he said, "I need to tell you something."

She lifted her head. "Oh, God. Is there *more?*"

"Plenty, but I've been thinking about this for two days, so I have to make sure I don't leave anything out." He smiled and laced his fingers with hers, turning their hands in a ray of sunshine. "See this?"

"What?"

"The light's turning everything to gold."

It did, she realized. It gilded their joined hands as it warmed them.

"That's sort of what happened," he said. "I started out with you looking for your father's lost gold, but along the way, I found something better. It had been right in front of me all the time, only I hadn't realized what I had until I almost lost it."

The past stirred, merely a hint of a shrug, then settled once more. Lydia's pulse started to race. "Derek, are you trying to tell me something?"

He laughed. "I'm doing a lousy job, but this is my first time, so bear with me."

"Your first time?"

"I've never told anyone that I loved them. You're my first."

The moment was too precious, as perfect as his kiss. She didn't want it to end. And she didn't want to miss any of it but her eyes were misting with tears, making the sunshine glitter.

And for the first time ever, the thought of gold didn't hurt. It hadn't been the source of the evil that had stalked her family. It was beautiful after all. As enduring as love.

Derek pulled her hand to his chest and tapped her fingers over his heart. "You're in here already. I thought I'd keep you out, but you've been there probably from the time you were sitting in my Jeep with half your hair dripping on your shoulders and the rest sticking straight out from your head in those crazy chunks. You pushed up your glasses and lifted your chin and looked so damn brave…" He closed his eyes and inhaled shakily, then looked at her. As the rising sun tipped his eyelashes with gold, his gaze was free from shadows and brimming with an honesty that went straight to Lydia's soul. "I love you, Lydia."

She spread her fingers, savoring his words. She felt as if she'd been trying to push at a door only to have it swing wide open. "Derek, I can't tell you when it started for me any more than I can tell you the first instant the sun started to rise. But I do know that I'll never love anyone the way I love you."

The next kiss wasn't gentle. It slammed through her exhausted body and her wrung-out emotions with a strength that made her heart soar. Here was the passion she'd expected, but it was richer, deeper than before.

She knew there was more to say. This was reality, not fantasy, and there were problems still to work out. Yet this was the first step. The rest would follow.

They left the blanket on the bench. They barely made it through the front door before they started ridding themselves of their clothes. Lydia gasped when she saw the bruises over his ribs and tried to soften her embrace, but Derek wouldn't let her. Kissing, touching, giddy with the release of tension, they stumbled naked down the hall. When her knees gave out, he carried her to his bedroom, laid her in the center of the mattress and pushed inside her.

Lydia quivered with the speed of her response. Without any preliminaries, a climax rippled through her body. She tilted her hips and locked her ankles behind Derek's waist, her nails digging into his shoulders as she felt him shudder. The wildness was what she needed, what they both needed. An affirmation of life in the most primitive sense.

She felt renewed, energized and delightfully *right,* as if she was exactly where she was supposed to be. If this was an adrenaline high, she could understand why it would be addictive.

"Whoa," Derek murmured, sliding his hands beneath her buttocks. Clasping her in place, he rolled to his back. "That was some rush."

She smiled, still trying to catch her breath. She checked for bruises, then stacked her hands on his chest and leaned her chin on her knuckles. "It was exactly what I needed. How do you always know?"

He grinned. "It's a gift."

"Mmm. That's one of the things I love about you, Derek. You're very good at this part."

"You're a quick learner."

She traced her finger along his lip. "I do love you."

"I can get used to hearing that."

"Good, because I plan…" She heard a distant trill of a phone and reflexively looked around. Most of the room was a blur—her glasses were somewhere in the hall along with her dress. "Is that your phone?"

"Relax," he said, tonguing her finger into his mouth. "There's no one I want to talk to except you."

She continued to look around. She hadn't been in Derek's room before. The decorating scheme was similar to hers, except the furniture was larger. She squinted at a shape near the wall and realized it was a suitcase. A duffel bag and a backpack sat beside it.

Some of the sensual haze she was drifting on began to fade. She pushed herself up. The suitcase was open and half full of folded clothes. The duffel bag and backpack appeared stuffed. "Derek, are you going some-where?"

He sat up, pulling her legs around his hips to keep her on his lap. "Anytime you're ready, my love."

Her breath caught as she felt him harden. She splayed her hands on his shoulders and tried to keep her train of thought. "No, I meant why are you packing? Tony's not evicting you now, is he?"

"I already talked to him. My debt's fully paid."

"Are you planning a tour so soon?"

"No. I'm packing because I'm moving out. Tony isn't taking the house, I'm giving it back to him."

"What?"

"Lydia, I'm selling my business. Someone else can run On the Edge Tours."

"But you worked so hard for it. You need it."

"Maybe at one time, but I don't anymore." He kissed her nose. "It's another one of those things I was look-ing for that I realize I had already found."

"What about your gambling addiction?"

"If it comes back, I'll get help." His gaze hardened as he focused on the bruise on her jaw where McAllis-ter had struck her. "I won't be able to build much of a life with you if I'm traveling all the time. I love you, Lydia. I'm not going to leave you."

She swayed into him, overcome by another wave of rightness. Everything was falling into place so perfectly, she was almost afraid to believe it. "You want to build a life with me?"

"Well, yeah. As I said, I'm new to this, but I think that goes with the whole love thing, doesn't it?"

She laughed and tilted her hips to fit herself more squarely on his lap. "It does, Derek. I want that, too."

"Great. How does moving back to Denver sound?"

"Denver?"

"Sandra said she'll pull some strings and get me back in the bureau."

The shocks just kept on coming.

Yet it wasn't really a shock, was it? She'd seen the yearning on Derek's face when he'd spoken of his old job. He'd wanted this all along. It wouldn't be easy to rebuild his reputation, but she already knew that Derek thrived on challenge. She sifted her fingers through his hair, taking care not to catch the bandage on his forehead. "I'm proud of you, Derek. I think that's wonderful news."

"Yeah, who would have thought?"

She kissed the bruised skin beneath his eye. "I would have. I've seen how the past can hold back the present. I'm glad you're putting yours to rest."

He wrapped his arms around her, rolled her to her back and started to move in a slow, easy rhythm. There was no urgency now—they had all the time in the world. "What you said before is true, Lydia. We do fit, and not just this way. Maybe fate did put us on the same road after all."

"Maybe it did," she murmured. "We both found what we hadn't realized we'd been looking for...." Something niggled in her memory. She saw a flash of gold in the darkness. It shone like a beacon, untarnished and enduring, lasting forever in a tribute to love.

And the final piece of the puzzle fell into place.

She gasped and clutched Derek's shoulders. "Oh, my God! I know where it is!"

He took her hand and moved it between them. "You mean this?"

She shuddered at a wave of pleasure. "Derek, I mean the gold."

He nuzzled the side of her neck. "Later."

"Derek—"

He nipped her earlobe. "Lydia, I don't want the gold," he said. "I want you."

Epilogue

Lydia laid the flowers in front of the wooden marker, then brushed the dirt from her knees and straightened up. Weather and years had worn off the names from most of the headstones in the tiny churchyard. The town had been left to the elements more than a century ago— little remained now except some crumbled foundations and the skeletal arch of a church window.

It was only one of the hundreds of ghost towns and abandoned settlements that were scattered across Arizona. Because it was too remote to be popular with tourists, it had been spared the ravages of vandals and souvenir hunters and so it appeared almost exactly as it had on the print that had hung in Zachary's study.

The picture in Lydia's memory, though, hadn't been

as clear because she'd seen the place through a haze of tears.

Derek moved behind Lydia and slipped his arms around her waist. "We could bring her home," he said. "Bury her beside your father."

She leaned her head against his shoulder. "I'd like that, Derek."

"I'll make some calls when we get back. We'll do it quietly."

"Thanks."

He kissed the top of her head. "Are you okay?"

"I am. I know they're both at peace."

"What about you?"

She folded her arms over his. "I'm at peace, too, Derek."

And in spite of the whirlwind of the past month, she was.

Hart McAllister had met justice, not from the courts but from a different power: less than two weeks after his arrest, he'd succumbed to a brain tumor. According to the medical examiner, the inoperable tumor had been growing for years and had possibly contributed to McAllister's behavior. In addition, his impending death likely had been a major factor in his drive to settle old scores.

But it wasn't McAllister's death that had left Lydia at peace, it was the life she and Derek were continuing to build. She glanced at the diamond that sparkled from her left hand. By this time next week, she would be married to Special Agent Derek Stone of the Denver FBI. Her new bookstore, funded by the sale of Derek's tour business, was scheduled to open three weeks after that. And although she and Derek had plenty of space in the modest house she and her father had shared, they were already talking about something larger for the day when they started their family.

Love, a family of her own. She could think of no better legacy. She moved her gaze to her mother's grave, then looked at the butte that rose on the far side of the valley.

That, too, was exactly as it had appeared on the print in her father's study.

A collage of memories blurred past as the ghost town fell behind and Derek steered the Jeep toward the butte, following the same route Lydia's father had taken twenty-four years earlier. It took them a while to find the right spot—bushes had grown over the entrance to the abandoned mine, concealing it completely from anyone who didn't know it was there. She and Derek eased the branches aside, careful not to break them, then switched on their flashlights and moved through the mouth of the tunnel.

The air was thick with the smell of age. The mine was older than the town. Timbers that had shored up the ceiling had long ago fallen and leaned crookedly against the walls amid piles of crumbled rock. The tunnel had been choked with debris the last time Lydia had been here, but now it was impassable.

She clasped Derek's hand and directed the beam of her flashlight through a gap in the timbers. The light moved over another dusty pile of rocks, but some of the rocks appeared too regular to be natural. Something glinted from the darkness. She angled her light downward and saw a flash of gold.

"That's got to be it," Derek said. He pitched his voice low, as if unwilling to disturb what had been laid to rest here. "From what I can see, the dimensions of that pile would be about right."

"That's it," she confirmed. "My father backed McAllister's truck as close as he could to the entrance, but it took him all night to carry the bullion inside. I sat over there." She pointed her light at a hollow in the wall. "I watched the whole thing. He didn't stop crying until he got rid of the last bar."

Derek squeezed her hand. "It wasn't any use to him."

"No, it wasn't. He'd only stolen it to save my mother. He loved her too much to keep any of it."

"What do you want to do?" Derek asked gently. "It's your call."

It was a fortune. Twelve metric tons. 170 million dollars.

But it couldn't compare to the treasure she'd already found.

Lydia looked at Derek. Even in the dimness of the tunnel, she could see his eyes gleam with his smile. "You already know what I want, don't you?"

"Yeah." He leaned down to kiss her. "I love you, Lydia. Let's go home."

* * * * *

Coming in November from

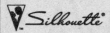
INTIMATE MOMENTS™

and author

Brenda Harlen
Dangerous Passions
IM #1394

With a hit man coming after her,
beautiful Shannon Vaughn was forced to
go on the run with Michael Courtland,
the sexy P.I. assigned to protect her. But
as the enemy closed in, Shannon realized
she was in greater danger
of losing her heart....

*Don't miss this exciting story...
only from Silhouette Books.*

Available at your favorite retail outlet.

INTIMATE MOMENTS™

Get ready for an emotional
adventure from
Marilyn Pappano:

The Bluest Eyes
in Texas

(#1391)
Available November 2005
From Silhouette Intimate Moments

Logan Marshall sought revenge upon the
man who murdered his parents, but instead
found private investigator Bailey Madison
on his trail. High adventure and deep
romance forced them into each other's arms
while searching for a stone-cold
killer who'd stop at nothing to stay
free…including killing again.

Available at your favorite retail outlet.

If you enjoyed what you just read,
then we've got an offer you can't resist!

Take 2 bestselling love stories FREE!

Plus get a FREE surprise gift!

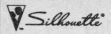

COMING NEXT MONTH

SIMCNM1005